THREE LAST FIRST DATES

COZY COTTAGE CAFÉ

KATE O'KEEFFE

WILD LIME BOOKS

ISBN-13: 978-1976434822
ISBN-10: 1976834823
Edited by Chrissy Wolfe at The Every Free Chance Reader

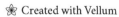

Wild Lime
Books

❀ Created with Vellum

ABOUT THIS BOOK

When it comes to men, Marissa Jones is totally committed to not being committed. One major heartbreak is enough for her.

Against her better judgment, Marissa agrees to a pact with her friends to marry the next guy she dates. But she isn't going to take any chances. For her, it's a numbers game, and one last first date just isn't enough. So, she ups the ante--three first dates with three very different guys, all in one day.

But can any of these men live up to her high standards?

Despite a few bumps in the road, from the three, she chooses The One. That is until the motorcycle-riding ex she never got over turns up, changing everything.

In the end, do you choose love or does love choose you?

ALSO BY KATE O'KEEFFE

It's Complicated Series:
Never Fall for Your Back-Up Guy
Never Fall for Your Enemy
Never Fall for Your Fake Fiancé

Love Manor Romantic Comedy Series:
Dating Mr. Darcy
Marrying Mr. Darcy
Falling for Another Darcy
Falling for Mr. Bingley (spin-off novella)

High Tea Series:
No More Bad Dates
No More Terrible Dates
No More Horrible Dates

Cozy Cottage Café Series:
One Last First Date
Two Last First Dates
Three Last First Dates
Four Last First Dates

Wellywood Romantic Comedy Series:
Styling Wellywood
Miss Perfect Meets Her Match
Falling for Grace

Standalone titles

Manhattan Cinderella

The Right Guy

One Way Ticket

CHAPTER 1

My name is Marissa Jones, and I'm totally committed to not being committed.

There, I said it. It was out there. No more pretending I was something I was not.

In fact, if I was going to be totally honest, I had a long and impressive history of avoiding commitment. I was the Commitment-Phobia Queen, if you will. And I was good at it. Really good. If you looked "commitment-phobe" up in a dictionary, I wouldn't have been at all surprised if you'd have found a photo of me, running away from some bewildered-looking guy as quickly as my heels could carry me.

That was why, when it came to dating, I was fussier than an OCD patient off their meds.

And why not? A girl had to have standards, right? Really, it's a matter of personal pride. I never expected to "settle" for someone, and nor did I want to. No way. No one but Mr. Absolutely Right would do for me.

Only problem was, I was hurtling towards thirty and I was having a hard time finding him.

That's why I agreed to a pact with my best friends to marry the next guy I dated. The One Last First Date Pact. It wasn't a trick name, it meant what it said. It meant no more messing around dating a bunch of different guys. No more wasted time on guys not worth our time. No more pointless flings or Mr. Right For Nows. It was going to be The One, or bust.

Which, in hindsight, for a commitment-phobe like me, was an off-the-charts crazy thing to agree to. Certifiable, really.

But something had to change. *I* had to change.

And, to be perfectly honest, I'd had more than my share of chardonnay that night and I hadn't really taken it all that seriously at the time.

But then "the thing" happened, something I barely even wanted to think about. That's when I knew I had to find The One. There was simply no more time to waste.

But, I wasn't taking any chances with this. Instead of going on a regular date with a guy the way my besties had, I decided to go on *three* dates in one day. Technically, I told my friends, it could be regarded as One Last First Date. They didn't buy it, but I decided to do it anyway.

The odds were good and I liked the math: one of me, three of them. It more than worked in my favor.

Not only that, I had thoroughly vetted each and every one of the three guys before I even threw on my outfit for the first date. If this was going to work—and I needed it to—I had to go in with my eyes wide open.

"I still can't believe you're doing this, Marissa," Paige said, shaking her head and smiling at me over our cups of coffee, what was left of our slices of cake in crumbs on our plates. "Three dates in one day? You're brave. Or insane."

"Why not? You and Cassie put all your eggs in one basket, and I don't want to do that. I figured going out with three different guys has *got* to improve the odds."

"Can you give us the lowdown on who these guys are? We need all the details, right, Cassie?"

"Oh, yes. Especially how good they look with their shirts off," Cassie added with a wicked grin.

"Well, I'm hardly going to find *that* out on a first date, but"—I raised my hand in the Girl Guides' salute—"I do solemnly swear to report all important details to you as they transpire."

"So? Details, Marissa," Cassie said, looking at me in expectation.

"Okay." I laid my hands flat on the table on either side of the empty dishes. "As you know, I'm going on three dates with three different guys all on the same day and they get to choose where we go and what we do."

Although I wasn't running a scientific experiment or anything, I had decided each guy would get to choose where we went and what we did on our dates. That way, I could get a clue as to what kind of people they were pretty quickly—and whether they were right for me. I mean, if one of them had said we were going to go to a chess tournament and then onto a war museum to see an exhibition of nineteenth century medals, I might have had second thoughts about dating him.

Paige clapped her hands together. "Oh, this is so exciting!"

I pressed my lips together. Exciting? Maybe. Terrifying? Definitely.

I swallowed down a lump in my throat, pushing my bobbed hair behind my ears. "Hmmm, we'll see."

"Just think, Marissa. One of those men is The One for you." Paige's face shone as I shifted uncomfortably in my seat.

Paige had always been the romantic one of our group of friends. She was the one who suggested the pact on the beach that night, the one who truly believed we all had a special person out there, just waiting to be found. Although she'd got the love speed wobbles not that long ago, she was now a fully carded member of Happy Coupledom and wanted everyone else to join the club, too.

"Well, he'd better be," I said, pushing my anxiety down. "I've put a lot of time and effort into vetting these guys."

And all I would say about that was social media was a wonderful invention for us would-be stalkers.

"Tell us about them," Cassie said.

"Well, the first guy I'm meeting is probably the wild card of the trio. His name is Coleman, and he's really smart and creative and interesting. He's Matt Damon."

3

I always liked to work out which Hollywood star the guys I dated resembled. If I couldn't find one, or much worse, the guy resembled someone like Danny DeVito, I didn't take things any further. Call me shallow, but I liked a guy to be easy on the eyes.

Was that a crime?

Coleman had Matt Damon's blue eyes and his hundred-watt smile, and although he was taller than his Hollywood counterpart, he had a similar kind of quiet confidence.

"Matt Damon, huh?" Paige said.

"Yup," I confirmed.

"So, why's he the wild card? Smart, funny, looks like Matt Damon. These are all good things, right?" Cassie asked, looking from me to Paige and back to me again.

"Yeah, it's his job that's kind of . . . out there," I replied.

"Oh? What does he do?"

"He's a . . . mortician." I held my breath, awaiting their reaction.

"What?!" Cassie and Paige shrieked in unison. Café patrons at neighboring tables turned to look at us.

I shot them a sheepish smile to reassure them I wasn't currently torturing my friends. "Settle down, you two. He's not all weird and creepy with it. He's a regular guy. He just does something out of the ordinary, that's all."

"What's out of the ordinary?"

I looked up to see Bailey standing beside our table, smiling down at us. She was dressed in her trademark Cozy Cottage Café red apron with white polka dots, matching the one Paige discarded to come sit with us fifteen minutes ago. They both ran the Cozy Cottage Café, our favorite hangout. With its welcoming atmosphere, comfortable seating, and large fireplace, it felt more like you were in someone's living room than a café in busy downtown Auckland. It was the perfect setting for our cozy catch-ups. As Paige had put it, it was our happy place.

"Want to take a seat for a second? Marissa's telling us about the dates she's going on this weekend," Cassie said.

"Oh, I wouldn't miss this for the world," Bailey said, pulling a chair from an empty neighboring table over to ours. "Paige? Is it okay if you keep an eye out for customers?"

"Of course," Paige replied.

Paige had only become joint owner of the Cozy Cottage with Bailey a matter of a few weeks ago, and already they had made a bunch of changes to the place, including opening on a Friday night for musical performances. In my more confident moments, I had been toying with asking them if they would allow me to sing one night, but I hadn't plucked up the courage to do so yet.

One day, maybe.

"What is this thing that's out of the ordinary?" Bailey asked as she flicked her dark curls behind her shoulder.

"Marissa's first date is with a mortician!" Paige said, with obvious delight.

Bailey tilted her head to the side. "Well, that *is* out of the ordinary. How exactly did you meet a mortician?"

"Actually, we met at the supermarket." I looked at my friends' open mouths. "Morticians eat too. Geez! Anyway, you know that urban myth about how if you have bananas in your shopping cart on a Tuesday you're telling others you're single?"

"Ah, no?" Cassie replied.

"Well, it's a thing. Trust me. So, he and I both had bananas in our baskets and he commented on how I had a larger bunch of bananas than he did and that it wasn't fair and he was going to call the Banana Police."

"Oh, how cute!" Paige said. "He's a flirt."

"He's a flirtatious *mortician*. That's kind of weird, Marissa," Cassie said.

I shrugged. "He's human; we flirted. Big deal. *Anyway—*" I flashed my interrupting friends a look, "—we flirted up a storm, right there in fresh produce. As you know, I'm a seasoned veteran when it comes to flirting." I grinned at my friends. It was true, I could flirt with the best of 'em. Although that's usually as far as it went, thanks to my commitment-phobia.

That was all about to change now, though.

"Where are you going on your date with this mortician?" Bailey asked.

"The *flirtatious* mortician," Cassie added.

I chose to ignore her. "We're meeting for brunch at Alessandro's, that swanky café downtown."

"So, not a cemetery?" Paige asked, elbowing Cassie.

Cassie giggled. "Or a morgue?"

"No," I said firmly. "Go on, get the jokes out of your system. But remember, this guy could be the one I marry and have children with, and you'll have to be nice to him then."

Of course, I got why they thought Coleman's job was weird. Heck, *I* thought it was weird. But really, it's just a job like any other—only with lots of dead bodies and sad people around you all the time.

"No more jokes, I promise," Cassie said as she tried to suppress a grin.

"Except, if Josh could make a shirt for him, I bet it'd say, 'Keep embalmed and carry on,'" Paige said, referring to her boyfriend's penchant for pun T-shirts.

I noticed Bailey's eyes sparkling as she pressed her lips together. "That one's funny, you have got to admit it, Marissa."

I shook my head good-humoredly and let out a sigh. "You three should be on the stage."

"I would have thought he would have gone for something a little more original than brunch at a café, though," Bailey added.

I shrugged. "It's what he chose."

"Right, so first up is Coleman the flirty mortician who looks like Matt Damon. Then who is it?" Paige asked, getting the conversation back on track. "I need to focus here. I've got to get back to work shortly. We can't spend all our time sitting around here, eating cake. Although, that does sound very appealing."

I raised my eyebrows. It was true, we had a thing for cake. We each had our favorites: Paige's was carrot cake with cream cheese frosting, Cassie's was the flourless raspberry and chocolate cake, and mine was orange and almond syrup cake. All delicious, all heavenly.

"Okay. Well, the next guy I'm dating is Nash."

"Nash, huh? Cute name. Where did you meet this one?" Paige asked.

"It's a nice story, actually. I was on my way to meet you for lunch a couple of weeks ago, remember, Paige?"

"Oh, yes! I remember you saying some guy had asked you out. The way it happened was so romantic." She put her hand to her heart.

"Nash is that guy. I walked past that construction site over on Jervois Road. You know the one, they've been working on that place for months."

"Oh, yeah, I do. The builders always whistle and call out when you walk past," Cassie said. "It's so annoying and embarrassing. I wish they wouldn't do that."

"I know, right? That's what happened to me. Only, Nash heard them doing it and yelled at them to be quiet. Well, he used other words than 'be quiet,' which I won't mention right now. They did what he said, and he jumped down onto the sidewalk next to me in his boots, took off his hard hat, and introduced himself to me."

"He sounds dreamy," Bailey commented, a whimsical look on her pretty face.

"Oh, yeah, he's definitely that," I replied, thinking of the way his hair was all flat when he removed his hat and how he ruffled it up with his fingers. "Dreamy" was the word for Nash, that was for sure.

"You like him the best," Cassie said, looking at me out of the corner of her eye.

My face warmed up, much to my annoyance. "Maybe. I don't know."

"Who's his Hollywood doppelgänger?" Bailey asked.

"Oh, that's easy. He's Jon Snow. Well, Kit Harington, the guy who plays Jon Snow. Only taller. He's got to be over six foot."

Bailey looked puzzled. "I'm sorry, you've lost me. Who's this Jon Snow person?"

Bailey had to be the only straight woman on the face of the planet who didn't know who the delectably dark, brooding, and oh-so manly Jon Snow was. "He's on *Game of Thrones*."

"Ah, you see, I've never watched it," Bailey replied.

7

"Yeah, I haven't either, but I know who Kit Harington is. Bailey, you need to borrow some of my trashy magazines," Cassie said. Turning to me, she asked, "Where is date number two?"

Before I had the chance to reply, Paige's chair scraped across the hardwood floor as she pushed herself up. "I want to hear everything, okay? Right now, duty calls."

I glanced over at the counter where two professionally dressed women were perusing the shelves of cakes, pastries, and the new line of pies Bailey and Paige had recently introduced. Those pies were doing nothing for my thighs, they were so good, and I'd extended my morning runs by an extra mile or two to compensate. "I'll fill you in. Go, run your café." I smiled at Paige, and she beamed back at me before she returned to the counter.

"I'm meeting Nash at Meola Reef," I said, naming a beautiful seaside park a few miles west of downtown Auckland. "All he said was to bring sensible walking shoes."

"Sensible walking shoes does *not* sound romantic, even if he does look like a tall Jon Snow," Cassie said, pursing her lips.

"I know," I said with a shrug. "But he's cute and I'm serious about making this whole Last First Date thing happen. I figured I'd give it a shot."

"Go in with an open mind," Bailey said with a smile. "And if it doesn't work out, at least you'll have something pretty to look at."

I laughed. "Exactly."

"So, that's Nash. Who's date number three? Wow, this feels like an episode of that old TV show, what was it called?" Cassie asked.

"*Blind Date?*" Bailey offered.

"That's the one. Behind curtain number one is a flirty mortician who likes to eat bananas," Cassie said with a theatrical wave, and I couldn't help but let out a giggle. She was right, this whole Last First Date thing was a little like being on a dating show. "Behind curtain number two, we have a construction worker who likes his women in sensible walking shoes." Cassie grinned. "And who do we have behind curtain number three?"

"A guy I met when I had to go to that swanky menswear place in the city to pick up a suit my stupid brother had ordered."

I thought of how my big brother, Ryan, had been sleeping on my sofa since his breakup with his girlfriend. He'd asked if he could stay for "a few nights." That was nearly four weeks ago, and he was *still* there, depressed and virtually permanently attached to my sofa.

"Does this man at the swanky menswear place have a name?" Bailey inquired, pulling my thoughts back to my Last First Dates.

"He's called Blaze," I replied, bracing myself for my friends' inevitable reactions. Blaze wasn't exactly a common name in Auckland, and they were bound to have a thing or two to say about it, knowing them.

Bailey raised her eyebrows, a smile teasing the corners of her mouth. "Blaze? Don't tell me he's a fireman. That would be too funny."

I shook my head. "He's not a fireman, but he could be. He's *hot* enough."

"Oh, no, you *didn't* just go there," Bailey said with a shake of her head.

I scrunched up my nose. "Yeah, I did. Actually, I found out his real name is Neville, so I can see why he goes by his nickname. Blaze is really cute and clearly works out. He's the brawn of the trio, that's for sure." I thought of his strong, broad shoulders and the bulging biceps I'd spied under his short-sleeved checkered shirt when I'd met him. My blush intensified.

"Brawny is good," Cassie said.

"Mm-hmm," Bailey confirmed. "Who's his Hollywood guy?"

"Matthew McConaughey. *Fool's Gold* Matthew, not *Gold* Matthew, of course. Right down to his messy blond hair and rippling muscles."

"Yum," Cassie said, and I noticed as everyone around our table appeared to take a moment, thinking about the delectable Mr. McConaughey.

"How do you manage to *meet* these guys?" Bailey asked.

"I don't know," I replied with a shrug. "Luck, I guess? But they're out there. You just need to look."

"You're really blushing now!" Cassie said, and immediately my cheeks heated up to positively nuclear proportions.

"No, I'm not," I replied, totally unconvincingly.

"Oh, yeah. He's your favorite, not Nash. It's Blaze all the way, baby," Cassie teased. "Now, what will you call your children, I wonder? Bonfire? Inferno?" She laughed heartily at her own joke as Bailey smiled at her, shaking her head.

I shot her a look. "Really, Cassie. I don't know why you don't just give up your day job and try to make it in comedy."

"After the material I've come up with today, I'm seriously considering it," she replied, her eyes dancing.

I laughed, knowing full well Cassie would never give up her job as Regional Sales Manager at AGD, the large telecommunications company we worked at together. She loved it too much, and as my boss, I would hate to see her go.

Who else would allow me to take a full hour off work on a Thursday morning to discuss men over cake?

"Where are you going with him?" Bailey asked.

"We've agreed to meet at O'Dowd's for a drink at seven," I said, naming the bar we regularly hung out at on a Friday night. "That way, we're going to a place I know."

"So, we could come along for that one? Hide out in the back or something?" Cassie asked.

"That's a great idea!" Bailey enthused.

I thought of how Paige and I had done just that when Cassie had gone on her Last First Date, and how we'd been witnesses to the dating disaster that unfolded before our eyes. "Actually, I think I'd prefer it if you didn't come—to *any* of the dates."

Cassie shrugged. "Okay, I guess." She shared a look with Bailey.

"Seriously, guys," I reiterated.

"How about we meet for a Three Last First Dates breakdown here on Monday?" Bailey suggested.

We all agreed, and Cassie and I said our farewells to Paige and Bailey, who were now both working hard behind the counter, serving their hungry customers. As Cassie drove through the city back to the

AGD offices, I gazed out the window at the buildings, the trees, and the pedestrians, ambling along the footpath, my mind full to the brim.

In two short days, I was going on the three most important dates of my entire life. Whether the men I was dating knew it or not, one of them was going to be my Last First Date.

And I was completely and utterly terrified.

CHAPTER 2

FIRST LAST FIRST DATE: COLEMAN

*S*aturday morning arrived and I was as ready as I would ever be for my three Last First Dates. Being the organized gal I was, I had googled what to wear on a first date and had created a Pinterest board of ideas. After a lot of different combinations, I had settled on a white loose-fitting top with a long necklace, a navy blazer, paired with some gray cropped skinny pants and strappy heels. I wanted to hit a balance between saying "this date is important to me" and at the same time "I'm totally relaxed about you, relationships, and everything." It was a surprisingly thin line, and one that had resulted in a pile of at least eight discarded outfits on my bed back in my apartment.

I arrived at Alessandro's a fashionable eight minutes late to meet my inaugural Last First Date, Coleman Adams. Eight minutes struck the right note between too early and too late. I spotted Coleman sitting at a table near the window as I passed by. He was clearly on the lookout for me, because the moment he spotted me he smiled, waved, and pushed his chair out to stand up.

As I rounded the corner and walked through the open door, I took in his T-shirt and jeans, the way his short, wavy hair was perfectly cropped. He had that Matt Damon grin the size of Texas plastered across his face, and as I arrived at the table, he greeted me with a "Hello," placing his hands on my arms and kissing my cheek. It was too sweet for words and the perfect start to our date.

"Wow," he said, his eyes skimming over me, making me tingle, "you look sensational, Marissa."

"Thanks, Coleman," I said, returning his grin, a couple of butterflies beating their wings in my belly.

This is starting out so well!

He pulled out a black leather chair for me—such a gentleman—and I sat down, thanking him. He positioned himself across the small, glass table, still watching me closely, still with that gorgeous grin on his face.

"I'm so pleased we're doing this," he said.

"Me too. Go the bananas!" I said, referencing the supermarket.

"Bananas are officially my new favorite fruit." His blue eyes crinkled as he held my gaze.

"Yeah, me too." My tummy did a little flip-flop. Maybe Coleman was The One?

"So, what do you want to eat?" he asked, breaking the spell by looking down at the menu in front of him. "It all looks great to me, but then I'm starving."

I picked up my menu and glanced down the page. There was the usual fare: pancakes, French toast, bacon and eggs. I decided on eggs Benedict almost immediately and returned my attention to Coleman.

"I'm having the full English: eggs, bacon, hash browns, the works," Coleman said as he placed his menu back on the table. "You?"

"Eggs bennie," I said with a shrug. "It's my usual."

"Your usual, huh? Maybe you should branch out, try something new?"

I thought about how I was looking for my Last First Date. This commitment-phobe couldn't get much more adventurous than that.

"You did say I got to call the shots on this date, right?" He raised his eyebrows flirtatiously at me, referring to my suggestion my dates today got to choose our activities so I could get to know them better.

"Okay, I will," I said with a small smile, collecting my menu and once again scanning the options. I landed on a delicious-looking dish. "I'm going to have the smashed avocado on toasted sourdough bread with a side of bacon and roasted tomatoes. That is, if it's okay with you?"

Coleman nodded at me. "Nice choice. I approve." A smile teased at the edges of his mouth.

He was enjoying being in control, that was for certain. Mental note: was this a good thing? I mean, *I* was the kind of person to take control, to make my own decisions, to choose my own path. The last thing I wanted was a man who thought he was in charge. No way, José.

But then, there was an outside chance I was overthinking this.

A waitress arrived at our table, and we placed our orders for food and coffee.

"And could you make the flat white extra hot with only about a seventh milk, not the usual fifth? Thanks."

I blinked at him as my mind began to whirr. I might be a little on the demanding side myself, but that was very prescriptive. A seventh as opposed to a fifth? *Hmmm.* Controlling *and* particular? If he was as particular about everything as he was about his coffee, what would that mean to be in a relationship with him?

"You need to use a guiding hand with these baristas, you know. I had this one coffee at a place on Hobson Street and, would you believe, they used skim milk instead of full fat? They thought I wouldn't be able to tell, but I could."

"Good for you," I said, watching him closely. In all the research I had done on Coleman, nowhere did it say "uptight about coffee." I liked a good cup of coffee as much as the next person, but wasn't he taking it all a bit far?

Argh! I needed to stop this! I knew exactly what was going on here, and I needed to give myself a stern talking to. I was doing what I always did: I was putting up barriers, talking myself out of having a relationship with a guy, rendering a date over before it had even had a chance to begin. And it needed to stop.

I could feel the rope in my belly begin to knot. *He's not The One.*

There was no way. He was too persnickety, too difficult, too . . .

"Marissa? Are you okay?" Coleman's concerned voice pierced my thoughts.

I forced a smile. "Yes, yes. Just listening to you and the . . . the coffee thing."

"Look, I know I can be a little intense about it, but I promise I won't be today."

He flashed his grin at me, and I relaxed a breath. "Okay, that sounds . . . great." I ran my fingers through my hair, forcing myself to move on from the coffee thing. "Now, tell me something interesting about you, something I don't already know."

"Well, I think you're cute," he replied, waggling his eyebrows up and down.

I couldn't help but laugh. "I said something I don't already know."

He laughed. "Busted."

I relaxed ten notches, letting out a breath. This was good. Flirting was good. *Not* talking about what fraction of milk to put in a cup of coffee was definitely good.

As I tossed my hair, I glanced behind Coleman and did a double take. Was that Cassie and her boyfriend, Will, at a table in the corner? I squinted, trying to make them out. The woman waved at me. Cassie. I pursed my lips. Having her here really added to the pressure.

". . . and I wondered if you'd like to see it?"

I shook my head, shooting Cassie a killer stare. "Sorry, what? I was distracted."

"I said, I've been working on something and I wanted to know if you would like to see it after this? It's the thing I had planned for us. I guess it's my way of showing you who I am."

"Sure. Great!" I focused all my attention on Coleman, trying my best to ignore Cassie and Will at the table at the back.

"Awesome."

As I smiled at Coleman, I noticed movement behind his head. Cassie was gesturing wildly at me. I glared at her, willing her to stop, but she was a woman on a mission.

"Would you please excuse me? I need to freshen up."

"Sure, of course." Coleman stood up as I did. I shot him an embarrassed smile. This guy was old-school polite! I kind of liked it.

I caught Cassie's eye and nodded at the ladies'. She jumped up from her table and followed me. Once the door was closed behind us, I turned to face her and crossed my arms. "Well? What are you doing here?"

Cassie gave a shrug. "I'm having brunch with my boyfriend. You just happen to be here, too."

I tapped my foot. "But you don't like Alessandro's. You said it's too slick and try-hard." I thought of the highly polished interior, with its mirrors, chrome, and black leather. It was about as far as a place could get from our preferred Cozy Cottage Café.

"Sometimes a girl wants a change of scene," she replied unconvincingly.

"And to spy on one of her friends on a date."

"Oh, come on! You can't blame me. I've never seen a flirty mortician before."

I softened, shaking my head. "Sure. I get it. Paige and I did it to you."

We grinned at one another.

"So, how's it going? He's really cute. Not at all what I'd expected."

"What had you expected exactly?"

"Not *him*, that's for sure. He's good-looking and young and *normal*."

"Of course, he's normal. Well, as normal as any of us are."

"I don't know, I guess I thought he'd have black hair and dark eye makeup, with tattoos of skeletons on his biceps, or something."

I knitted my eyebrows together. "Cassie, you're thinking of a Goth."

"Oh, yeah. I guess I am. Huh. He's not that, though. I think you make a really cute couple."

"Thanks." I smiled, and I turned to check my makeup in the mirror. As I wiped a small smudge of mascara from under my left eye, an image of Coleman dressed as a Goth popped into my head. I pushed it away immediately.

"I'll leave you to your date," Cassie said, her hand on the door.

"So, you're not going to pop up at my next two dates?" I asked.

"Maybe? I mean, we need to have the full information, you know?"

I shook my head as I smiled at her reflection in the mirror. "You're impossible."

"Yes, and you love me for it." She flashed me a grin before she disappeared, the door closing quietly behind her.

Back at the table, the waitress had delivered our orders already.

"Wow, that was fast," I commented as I sat down in the chair Coleman had pulled out for me once more.

"That's one of the many reasons why Alessandro's is my favorite café in Auckland," Coleman said, taking his own seat.

I thought of the Cozy Cottage. With its warm ambience and homey feel, it left this place for dust. A moment later, I held my breath as Coleman lifted his coffee cup to his mouth. I watched as he took a sip.

"Well?" I asked, not sure if I wanted to hear his verdict.

"Passable." His face broke into a smile. "Good, actually."

I let out a puff of air. "I'm pleased to hear it."

We ate our meals and chatted. Every now and then he would throw in a flirty comment and I would flirt right back, enjoying our repartee. He was cute, he was fun, he was clearly into me. I had over-reacted before, doing what I do. This. This was good.

And then he mentioned his job.

The sum total of my experience of morticians was meeting one at my grandmother's funeral last year and watching the TV show, *Six Feet Under*. As I looked at Coleman, sitting opposite me, sipping his coffee and talking about his life, I wondered if he ever had imaginary conversations with the recently deceased? And if so, what did they find to talk about?

I shook my head. I needed to look past things like that, to see Coleman for who he was, not some ridiculous stereotype. Sure, he was a mortician, but it should really be no big deal. It's not like he was his job—his job was merely his job.

So, why did I keep imagining him dressed in black with a top hat

17

and gray pallor to his face, skeleton tattoos on his arms, applying makeup to dead people lying in coffins with spooky music playing in the background?

Damn Cassie, putting that idea into my head!

I cleared my throat. "Do you like your job?"

"I don't want to boast, but I put the 'fun' in 'funeral,'" he replied with one of his flirty grins.

I wrapped my arms around my body. Did he really just say that?

"Do you get it? 'Fun in funeral'?" he asked, his eyes dancing, as though I had somehow missed his joke.

"Yes, yes, I get it," I replied, forcing a smile.

"Sorry. I sometimes forget funerals aren't regular people conversation."

"That's fine. I just . . . my granny died last year, and the funeral was pretty hard."

He rearranged his features into the face of concern. "I can imagine." He put his hand on mine. It was warm and reassuring, and I felt myself loosen up.

I cleared my throat and decided to take the bull by the horns. I needed to get over this whole mortician thing so we could move forward. "Have you always been a mortician?"

He nodded. "I had a near-death experience as a teenager. I had never thought I'd enter the family business, but when I nearly died, it kind of came to me: this was what I was born to do. It was my calling, I guess."

I looked at him, aghast. "What happened when you were a teenager?"

"I was one of those idiots who thought he could drive as fast as he liked after a few beers. I ended up wrapping my car around a lamppost and having to be cut out to get to hospital. I thanked God I didn't have any passengers, and I learned my lesson good that day."

"No more drunk driving?"

"No more drinking, period."

"Oh."

"That event spelled the end of my teenage rebellion. As soon as I recovered, I went back to school, graduated, and entered the family business. You see, us Adams have been in 'the business,' as we call it, for three generations now. My grandpop set up Adams Funeral Homes back in the sixties."

I nodded encouragingly at him. *They are not the Addams Family. They are not the Addams Family.*

"We're kind of *The Addams Family*, I guess, only with one *d*," he added with a chuckle.

Noooo!

"Shall we get the check? I want to show you that thing I mentioned."

"Sure, that sounds great." Anything was better than picturing Coleman as Uncle Fester, the theme song ringing in my ears.

A few moments—and a surreptitious thumbs-up from Cassie—later, Coleman offered to drive me. Although I had researched him online and knew a little about his family and friends, his hobbies and his job, I had no clue whether he was a psychopath or serial killer. I mean, you would hardly advertise the fact on social media if you were, would you?

I decided it was best to be cautious—plus, it gave me a chance to try to kill off those mortician-related road blocks I kept throwing in our way. No pun intended.

"How about I follow you? My car is parked just over there." I pointed across the road where I had miraculously found a space— miraculous because parking was at a premium in the city, and finding a space near where you actually wanted to be was like finding a hen's tooth in a haystack. Or was I mixing my metaphors there?

"Funny! You're parked right next to me. What are the chances?"

I glanced at the car parked behind mine. It was large and shiny and black, virtually screaming "I transport dead people!" I swallowed.

Coleman surprised me by taking my hand in his, and we walked across the street together. I heard the *blip blip* of a red sports car parked in front of mine and snapped my head to look at Coleman in surprise.

He flashed me his grin. "Don't judge me."

I returned his smile, relief flooding me. He didn't drive the death mobile! He drove a sexy red sports car! I could have hugged him.

"Follow me."

I climbed into my hatchback and started up the engine. It was time for a good talking to. So far, Coleman had been wonderful. He was a total gentleman, he was flirty and fun and interested in me, and he wanted to show me something that would help me understand who he was. I *had* to stop my mind messing with me. He was a nice guy, and I was lucky to be on a date with him.

I followed him through the city streets, through Newmarket, and onto the busy motorway. A few exits later, we left the motorway and drove through a leafy suburb. We pulled into a carpark at the back of a weatherboard building.

I stepped out of my car, looking around. Although it was clearly the back of a building, it was beautifully landscaped, with a row of magnolias on both sides of the carpark, a border of lavender, and a perfectly manicured hedge completing the look.

"Hey," Coleman said, smiling at me as I locked my car.

"Hey," I echoed, returning his smile, the butterflies back in my belly.

Our date was back on track.

"I'm really excited to share this with you," he said, running his hand down my arm and taking my hand in his.

"I'm really excited you want to," I replied. We stood looking at one another for a beat, two.

It felt nice; it felt right.

"Now, when we go in I need you to forget what it is and just appreciate it for its beauty, all right?"

"Okay." I nodded at him as my hand got clammy. "Is this . . . is this your funeral parlor?"

"It sure is," he said with obvious pride.

Suddenly, I was having a tough time not seeing Coleman as Peter Krause in *Six Feet Under*. Will any of the dead bodies sit up and talk to me?

He let go of my hand and unlocked the back door. Swinging it open, he stood back for me to enter.

"Thank you," I muttered. I slunk inside.

As Coleman banged the door shut behind me, I almost jumped out of my Nine Wests. I took a few deep breaths in an attempt to quell my nerves. Come on! I was being ridiculous! I was simply visiting Coleman's workplace, a workplace like any other. It was no big deal.

Only . . . there weren't any dead people where *I* worked.

"Come through here." Coleman pushed a heavy, stained wooden door open, and I was genuinely surprised it didn't creak in a sinister way.

He held the door open for me once more, and I walked into a dimly-lit room, seriously beginning to question my sanity. Sure, I'd researched him on social media and found out what I could about him, and he seemed like a nice guy. But I didn't know him, not really. This was our first date, after all. What was I doing here? Why had I gone to a *second location* with him, the one thing you're not meant to do? What was he going to do to me? What was . . .

Coleman flicked the light switch, and the room was instantly flooded with bright light. I glanced around, taking in the workbench, the tools, the wood shavings on the floor.

"This is what I wanted to show you," Coleman said as he took a few short strides over toward a bulky item, covered with a gray tarpaulin in the center of the room. He took the corner in his hand and tugged, the light fabric of the tarpaulin slipping down to the ground in one graceful movement.

My mouth slackened, and my eyes almost popped out of their sockets. Coleman was beaming with pride, standing next to an ornate coffin. It looked like it was only half finished. One end was rough and could give you splinters if you touched it, and the other was intricately carved into a beautiful pattern of what appeared to be climbing roses.

"I've been working on this for weeks. I'm hoping to start a line of these for the home. Kind of like the luxury end of the market."

There was a luxury end in death? I took a step back as every thought, every red flag, every one of my fears reached a crescendo in my brain. Coleman was a mortician, and his hobby was to work on coffins.

I couldn't breathe. I had to get out of here!

Coleman looked at me questioningly. "Are you okay, Marissa? You look . . . weird."

I opened my mouth to speak, but no words came out. Instead, as I took another step away from Coleman and his coffin, I bumped into the open door, making me leap.

"I . . . I have to go," I managed as I fumbled for the doorknob. Finding it, I pulled the door open and, without a backward glance, turned on my heel. I fled out the door, down the hallway, toward the exit. As I reached the door to freedom, I yanked it open and got my shoe wedged between the door and the wall. I wrestled with it, trying to break it free, but it was stuck.

Despite my thudding heart, banging in my ears, I could hear foot-steps behind me.

"Marissa?" Coleman called out.

I turned and looked into his bemused face as I wrenched my foot out of my shoe. "Sorry," I muttered. I took two steps out the door and pulled it closed behind me. Panicked and wearing only one shoe, I rummaged through my purse for my keys, finding everything but: a packet of tissues, my lipstick, a shopping list, a hair tie. Finally, my fingers felt something metal, and I yanked my keys out with shaking hands, hearing the satisfying *blip blip* of my car unlocking.

I grabbed hold of the door handle, pulled it open, and dived in. I glanced up and saw Coleman, standing in the doorway, watching me, looking like he had absolutely no idea what had just happened.

After three attempts to get my key in the ignition—why did they make the hole so *small?*—I started the car, banged it into gear, and hightailed it out of there with my tires squealing like a hoard of unhappy piglets.

A flirty mortician who carved coffins for fun was clearly a step too far for Marissa Jones.

CHAPTER 3

SECOND LAST FIRST DATE: NASH

I had managed to calm myself down, pushing thoughts of coffins, death, and Coleman—in no particular order—right down into the deep recesses of my mind before I got out of my car to meet date number two for the day.

When I'd reached my apartment after my hasty retreat, my nosy and annoying older brother, Ryan, had quizzed me on my date.

"That sounds like it totally sucked," he'd said with a chuckle as he plopped himself down on the sofa next to where I had been trying to recover from my ordeal.

"Not the best," I'd replied, crossing my arms defensively.

"Ah, sis. Sorry about that."

I rolled my own. "Sure, you are."

I was about as convinced as my high school math teacher when I'd told her my completed homework assignment had "accidentally" fallen into the blender with a handful of blueberries and yogurt.

"No, I am. Really. Of course, finding that happily ever after you and your friends are looking for is never going to happen. But still, you don't want a bad date."

Had I mentioned my brother had become a total cynical pain in the ass since his breakup?

In my car, I pushed Ryan's negativity out of my head. He may have been in a "relationships suck" state of mind, but I was looking for Mr. Right, and I wasn't going to let him drag me down.

I glanced at my watch. I had a few minutes to spare before I met my second Last First Date. I pulled my phone out of my purse and pressed the Facebook app. I bit my lip. *Should I check it?* Before I could stop myself, I typed in "Eddie Sutcliffe," my belly flip-flopping the instant his gorgeous smiling face filled my screen. I pressed "About" and scanned the screen. When my eyes settled on the words "Engaged," I quickly switched my phone off and slipped it back in my purse.

No change there.

I checked my reflection in the mirror and climbed out of my car. A second Last First Date called for a new outfit, and I was dressed in my favorite pair of skinny jeans, a cute pink T-shirt, a floppy hat on my head to protect me from the summer sun, and the "sensible shoes" my date had asked me to wear.

After a short walk, I arrived at the seaside park we were due to meet at. I looked around. The place was full of people with their happy, yappy dogs, throwing sticks and balls. I smiled to myself. They were having the time of their lives, running, jumping, playing. I watched a newly arrived dog run over and sniff another dog's butt. They were so obvious in their interest in one another: no subterfuge, just a straight out "I want to sniff your butt. Want to sniff mine?" approach, where every dog knew where she or he stood.

Why couldn't it be as simple for us humans? Not that I was into butt sniffing or anything, you understand.

I scanned the park, looking for Nash Campbell, Mr. Construction Worker, my second date of the day. The good news was, however, there was no sign of Cassie, Paige, or Bailey here. That was a good sign: I could have this second date of the day in peace and quiet.

"Marissa!" I heard a voice call. I looked over to a group of beautiful pohutukawa trees in full bloom—New Zealand's Christmas tree, as they were known, thanks to their red flowers appearing in December

THREE LAST FIRST DATES

each year. I spotted Nash waving at me beneath them, a grin on his Jon Snow face.

I waved back and navigated my way through the dogs and their owners, reaching his side a few moments later.

"Hey," he said, grinning from ear to ear. He put his hand on my shoulder and kissed me on the cheek. That was two cheek kisses today and counting.

"Hi, Nash," I replied, returning his grin.

"Looking good!" he exclaimed, taking in my casual attire. "I like the jeans and T-shirt thing. It's great to see you out of your clothes," he said.

I shot him a quizzical look. Did he really just say it was good to see me naked? I glanced down at my T-shirt. No "Nipplegate" situation, nothing where it shouldn't be. I looked back up at him, my brows knitted together.

His grin dropped. "No no no no no. I mean, it's not that I want to see you without your clothes on . . . well, I do, but . . . you look good in *different* clothes. That's what I mean." He scrunched up his face, regarding me through squinted eyes.

"Err, thanks?"

He laughed, shaking his head. "I'm pretty smooth, aren't I?"

"'Smooth' is probably not the word I'd use, but you're cute, so you can get away with it."

"Cute is good. I'm happy with that."

I smiled at him. He must be nervous. Either that or I hadn't noticed he could put his foot so firmly in his mouth when we'd met that day outside the construction site.

"Shall we start again?" he asked, his face hopeful.

Before I had the chance to reply, a dog shot past me, clipping me with his tail. "Ow!" I called out, more from shock than pain.

"Dexter!" Nash yelled in a loud voice beside me, making me jump. I watched as the whippy-tailed black dog stopped in his tracks, turned, and came bounding over toward us, his tongue hanging out of the side of his mouth. He looked like he was in complete and utter doggy heaven.

"Good boy," Nash said, squatting down next to him and patting him firmly on the side, Dexter's tail wagging so hard it could spin off. Nash looked up at me and said, "This is Dexter. Dexter meet Marissa."

I wasn't quite sure what the protocol was when meeting a dog, so I gave him a tentative pat on the head and said, "Hello, Dexter." The dog butted my hand and proceeded to lick it before I had the chance to steal it away, leaving a slick of dog slobber on my palm.

Nash didn't seem to notice—or care. "He likes you."

"Great," I replied, wishing I'd thought to bring some hand sanitizer.

Nash straightened up. "Here," he said, holding a long, hot pink plastic stick with a tennis ball sitting in a holder at the end. "Take this and throw."

"Okay." I took the stick and noticed as Dexter's excited attention was immediately directed at me. I had seen these things before, but never actually used one. Dexter's eyes were trained on me as though he and I were the only creatures on the face of the planet—which could almost be romantic if it wasn't for the fact Dexter was a *dog*. I raised the stick behind my head and threw it with all my might. As soon as it was out of my hand, Dexter darted after it. I turned to Nash, happy with my efforts.

"Ah, you're not meant to throw the whole thing," Nash said, shaking his head. "Just the ball."

I bit my lip. "Oh." So, now it was my turn to be humiliated? I looked over on the grass to where Dexter was pawing at the ball, still stuck in the ball holder at the end of the stick. "Sorry."

"No worries," Nash said, walking toward Dexter. He picked the contraption up and threw the ball. I watched as it sailed through the air, Dexter sprinting after it, expertly avoiding any people or dogs in his path.

"You're not a dog person, are you?" Nash said.

I shrugged. "Actually, I really like dogs, it's just I haven't had one since I was kid. I'd like to again one day, though." I watched a couple of small, fluffy dogs dart around one another, yapping excitedly, and couldn't help but smile. "Dexter seems . . . nice."

Nash chuckled, clearly recovered from his "It's good to see you out of your clothes" comment earlier. "He certainly is 'nice,' as you put it. He's a rescue dog."

"Oh? Wow." I had a sudden image of Nash, dressed in sexy mountaineering clothes, finding Dexter as a sweet little puppy, cowering under a rock, and my heart melted.

"You see that's why I wanted to bring you here. Dex is a really big part of my life, and I'm involved in a dog rescue organization."

"That's so great," I said, looking at Nash through fresh eyes. Sure, I'd known he was into dogs from his social media profile, but this was his passion. And it looked good on him.

"Thanks," he beamed at me. "Dex was my first dog, but I've got some more right now, too."

"More?" I asked, my eyebrows raised in alarm. "How many, exactly?"

"Well, there's Gretel. She's at home."

"Okay. So, you have Dexter and Gretel."

Two dogs? That seemed reasonable to me. Not weird. I'd had enough weird for one day.

"And there are the puppies, too." Dexter dropped the ball at Nash's feet. He picked it up with his ball holder and threw it again, the dog scampering after it.

"You have puppies?" I put my hand to my chest. "Aw! I love puppies. How many?"

"Five."

Back up the bus, Nash had *seven* dogs? Was it just me or was that a little over the top, perhaps even dog-obsessive?

"Wow, you must go through the slippers," I said, unsettled.

Was there such a thing as a weird dog guy, like there was a weird cat lady?

He chuckled. "Yeah."

"So, you like dogs, huh?" I said, trying to push the idea of Nash being some kind of bizarre dog-obsessive from my head.

Of course, I knew the answer to this question. I had stalked him, after all. And then there was the fact he had *seven* dogs. If he didn't like them, he'd have to be a special kind of weird.

Nash furrowed his brow. "Yes," he replied as though I hadn't noticed we were a) at a dog park with his dog, and b) he'd just told me about his gaggle of canines.

Right on cue, Dexter bounded over to us and dropped the slobbery old tennis ball at Nash's feet once again. In one fluid movement, he scooped the ball up in the ball holder and threw it. And this routine was repeated again, and again, and again.

"What got you into rescuing dogs?" I asked after an awkward silence in which I tried not to think about how bad Nash's house must smell. I mean, five puppies? Don't they need to be house-trained? There must be puppy poop and pee *everywhere*. Euw!

"I grew up with dogs, so I've always loved them. A while back, I decided I wanted to do something more meaningful than managing construction sites. Don't get me wrong, I like my job, but I *love* dogs, and I'm happy to help them out any way I can."

The way he put it didn't make him sound weird at all. In fact, I liked it. "You have a passion and you're pursuing it. I admire that. A lot of people spend their whole lives not following their passion."

He threw the ball—yet again—for Dexter, regarding me out of the corner of his eye. "What's the passion you're not pursuing?"

Momentarily surprised at such a direct question, particularly from a man holding a large hot pink ball throwing device in his hand, I bumbled my reply. "Oh . . . umm . . . nothing much."

He turned to face me. "Come on, there must be something."

My tummy tied into a knot. There *was* something, but I hadn't talked to anybody about it before. I pulled a face, hoping he'd get the message.

He didn't. "Shall I guess?"

I shrugged.

"You want to run off and join the circus so you can share your lion-taming skills with the world."

"Close, but no banana," I replied with a small smile.

"Oh, I've got it! You've got your name down for reassignment surgery, just waiting to become 'Malcolm'?"

I whacked him playfully on the arm. "No! And thanks a lot."

He shrugged. "I'm just trying to make up for that whole embarrassing thing about your clothes earlier," he replied.

I sniggered, enjoying the feeling of closeness our banter was generating. "By suggesting I want to be a man?"

"Hey, it's *your* passion, honey. I'm just trying to work out what it is since you refuse to tell me."

Softening, I replied, "If I tell you, will you promise not to share it with anyone and drop the whole 'Malcolm' thing?"

"I promise." He placed his hand over his heart, and I immediately noticed the outline of his firm pecs under his T-shirt. I bit my lip.

Not bad, not bad at all.

Before I had the chance to back out, I said, "I want to sing." I waited for his response, wondering why I was opening up to this guy so early on in the date—but liking it at the same time.

"Sing, huh? As in join a choir type of singing or go on *The Voice?*" he asked.

"Neither. Just . . . sing."

"That sounds straightforward enough to me. In the shower, maybe?"

"Are you going back to that whole 'naked' thing, again?" I joked, although this time it was fun, a little *risqué*, as the French would have it.

Nash threw the ball for Dexter—would this game ever get old for that dog?—and looked off into the distance. "Hmm, let me think. Marissa singing in the shower."

Again, I whacked him playfully on the arm. "Enough, already!"

"Sorry, but you are super hot and I am just a man."

I shook my head, laughing. *This is going so well!* Nash was cute and fun and flirty, and all the things I had hoped in a Last First Date.

Other than the dog slobber, that was.

"What's stopping you?" he asked, punctuating my thoughts.

"Singing in the shower? I already do that!"

"No," he said with a chuckle, "what's stopping you pursuing singing, like say, for an audience?"

Me, was the simple answer. I hadn't always been the slim, confident woman I was today. No way, José. Not too many years ago, guys like Nash and Coleman and Blaze wouldn't have given me a second glance. I was shy, totally lacking in confidence, and I was a little on the plump side of the equation. Heck, who was I kidding? I was F. A. T. fat. And I hated it. Some women embraced their size, loving their curves. Like Bailey. She was curvy and looked like some sort of Italian screen goddess from the fifties. Not me. I had been a major comfort eater, and every time I looked in the mirror, I wanted to slap my chubby face. Hard.

Then, once I'd graduated high school and was studying at college, I decided it was time I changed—no one was going to do it for me. I didn't want to spend my life hating what I saw. So, I got into running and I cleaned up my diet. There was no overnight, miraculous change, no "big reveal." It was gradual, my mindset about myself changing slowly as my body became stronger, healthier. I began to like what I saw when I looked in the mirror.

But, to this day, I still knew, deep inside of me, that shy, overweight, unhappy girl lay dormant, ready to rear her head.

Rather than delving into my most private of thoughts about myself, in response to Nash's question about what was stopping me, I simply shrugged and said, "I don't know."

"Then there's nothing standing in your way, right?"

Ah, if only it were that easy.

"I guess. So," I began, changing the subject quick-smart, "shall I give the throw-y thingamajig another try?"

"Sure. It's called a 'ball thrower,'" he said, his fingers in quotation marks, "on account of the fact it throws a ball."

I shook my head. "Very funny."

Dexter dropped the slimy, utterly gross, discolored ball at Nash's feet once more. I leaned in front of him and scooped it up with the ball thrower, Dexter's attention immediately focusing on me. This time, when I threw the ball, I held onto the pink stick and watched as the ball flew through the air, Dexter scrambling at a rate of knots across the park in hot pursuit.

"Nice," Nash said, watching the ball. "That one might make it to the sea."

"Well then, let's hope your dog can swim."

Nash chuckled. "Do you want to have some lunch? We can head to my local. They know Dex there."

After the brunch I'd had earlier in the day with Coleman the flirty mortician—wow, that was *today?*—I hadn't thought I would be hungry for hours. But my tummy rumbled at the mention of lunch, and I had really enjoyed the date with Nash so far, so I nodded with a smile. "That sounds wonderful."

Nash called Dexter, and we ambled through the park and onto the sidewalk. "I'm parked over there," I said, pointing at my car. "Where should we meet?"

"You can park at my place, and we can walk from there." He gave me his address, and I realized he lived only a few blocks from my apartment building.

A short drive later, I parked behind Nash's pickup truck in his driveway. I couldn't help but check his house out: a cute restored cottage, painted dark blue with white trim and a gabled roof. The guy had style.

I checked my makeup in the rearview mirror and quickly freshened up my lipstick before jumping out of the car and greeting Dexter once more. He acted like I was his long-lost friend, returned from the dead.

Nash chuckled. "You have a new fan."

I patted Dexter as he leaned against my legs, marveling at how comfortable I felt with this large, slobbery dog—and his owner. "I guess I do."

Nash clipped a lead on Dexter's collar, and we walked together down the street toward his "local," Dexter trotting calmly at Nash's side.

"Have you lived in this neighborhood long?" I asked as we passed familiar stores and cafés.

"I bought a house and renovated it. So, yeah, a while. I really like it here, although it'd be great to have more space for the dogs."

From my research prior to our date, I knew Nash was thirty-two: a very marriageable age, which, of course, was one of my considerations when I was choosing whom to date. I knew he had lived here for years, and I was surprised I hadn't seen him on the weekends.

"Here we are," Nash said as we drew to a stop outside Ready to Eat, a café I had eaten at only a month or so ago. It had large windows, overlooking the street, with an oversized blackboard where a talented member of staff had drawn a picture of some fantastical beasts and mermaids, all in colorful chalk.

"Oh, I love this place! Good choice."

We walked past the tables on the street and through the open door. Nash was instantly greeted with an enthusiastic "hello" from a hipster guy with a bushy beard behind the counter.

"How are you doing, Bojan?" Nash asked him as the men shook hands over the top of the counter.

"Great, man. You?"

"Awesome, as always. Hey," he said, turning to me, "this is Marissa."

Bojan extended his hand and I shook it. "Nice to meet you, Bojan."

"Likewise," he said with a grin. He let go of my hand and said, "Hey, Dexter! How you doing, boy?"

Dexter's tail immediately started banging against my leg.

"You here for lunch?" Bojan asked us.

"We are indeed."

"Cool. Grab some menus and I'll come take your order. Your usual table is reserved."

His usual table? Nash clearly thought the first part of our date would go well enough for us to make it this far. I smiled to myself. I admired his confidence.

We walked through the café and out the back door to an area I never knew existed, although I had been here a handful of times. It was a tiny courtyard with only a few tables, all wrought iron with chairs with comfortable cushions. There was a pergola with ivy climbing up its sides and overhead, dappling the light beautifully.

32

"This place is gorgeous!" I exclaimed.

"I thought you'd been here before."

"Never to this part."

"You've been missing out, then. Here." He gestured to a small table for two with a "reserved" sign in its center, and we sat down, Dexter arranging himself at Nash's feet.

A moment later, Bushy Bearded Bojan appeared at our table, menus and glasses of water in his hands, which he proceeded to place on the table. "We've got that halloumi, rocket, and fig stack with sourdough bread again, Nash."

Nash looked at me, his eyes bright. "You've got to try that."

I narrowed my eyes at him. A halloumi, rocket, and fig stack sounded a little feminine for a guy who looked like he worked out, but then, maybe I wasn't giving him credit for being a foodie. "That sounds great." I looked up at Bojan, marveling at his beard. I mean, it was nicer than some women's hair. "I'll have the halloumi stack and a skinny latte, thanks." I handed him my menu.

"Me too," Nash said, following suit. "Oh, with a side of steak." He winked at me, and I shook my head.

And there it was.

Beginning to feel very relaxed and comfortable with him, we chatted about ourselves, enjoying the warm outside air and the quaint surrounds. And we got on really, really well. Unlike the first date of the day—which still made me shudder whenever it crept into my mind—I was finding it hard to latch onto anything bad about Nash at all.

Which was extremely surprising for someone with a degree in fussiness.

By the time we had finished our lunch, I was almost completely convinced Nash would be the winner of the day. Although I had one more date to go on, I simply couldn't imagine enjoying anyone's company as much as I had Nash's.

"Hey, this was fun," he said as we left the café and walked slowly back toward my car. He slipped his free hand in mine, and I looked up into his eyes and smiled. It felt good; it felt right. We ambled the couple of blocks to his house, stopping beside my car.

"Thank you for a really nice day," I said, suddenly awkward.

Now would be the perfect moment for us to have our first kiss—perhaps my last ever first kiss—and the magnitude of the moment had a couple of hamsters scuttling around in my belly.

"I had a great time," Nash said, taking a step closer to me so we were almost touching. He ran his hands down my arms, and I knew this was it, our first kiss. My heart rate kicked up a notch—or ten.

Our attention was diverted by Dexter letting out a long whine. Nash laughed, breaking the spell. "He's jealous!" he said, crouching down to pat Dexter, who lapped up the attention.

I wondered if Dexter was having a canine fantasy of dispensing of me so he could have Nash all to himself.

"You're a good boy, Dex," Nash said to him, still crouching down next to his dog and holding his face in his hands. "You're still my number one."

And then, I watched in horror as Dexter's long tongue darted out of his mouth, planting a wet, slobbery lick, right across Nash's face. It was like everything had gone into slow motion, but there was nothing I could do to stop it.

The moment Nash straightened up and pulled me into him once more, I stiffened. Was Dexter's slobber on Nash's lips? Perhaps even in his *mouth*?

And I could tell you one thing, dog slobber was not sexy.

As Nash leaned back in to kiss me, I held my breath, pressing my lips together, bracing for the transferal of dog slobber from one human to another. I had to work hard to resist the urge to gag.

His lips brushed my clenched upper lip in possibly the least sexy kiss of all time.

He pulled away from me, a confused look on his face, a face, in that moment, I could not believe I thought once looked like Jon Snow.

"What was that?" he asked.

I swallowed. "Nothing. You're great. And your dog? He's great. You're both great." Nash was watching me with clear confusion. "I . . .

I just have to go. Sorry. I didn't realize what the time was, and I have a thing I need to get to."

I couldn't look at him, instead I focused my attention on locating my keys in my purse, an uncomfortable sense of *déjà vu* washing over me. I hit the "open" button and fumbled behind myself for the door handle.

Nash took a step back, watching me closely through narrowed eyes. "You have to go?"

Locating the handle and yanking open the door awkwardly behind me, I said, "Yes, sorry. I'll . . . I'll call you."

Although, I knew I had no intention of doing *that* anymore.

I turned and opened the door fully, climbed into the car, and slammed the door shut. I resisted the strong urge to hit the "lock" button, instead starting the car up and throwing it into gear. I gave him a tight smile and waved like I was a child waving at a clown on a float, and began to back out of the driveway.

As I turned onto the street, I looked back at Nash standing next to a seated Dexter with his arms crossed, his brows knitted together in confusion. I waved once more and put my foot down, leaving Nash, Dexter, and their combined saliva behind.

CHAPTER 4

THIRD LAST FIRST DATE: BLAZE

*"W*hich one are you going to pick?"

I chewed the inside of my lip, my partially eaten orange and almond syrup cake sitting on a plate on the table in front of me. I looked out of the Cozy Cottage Café window at the street, watching as cars and pedestrians passed by.

I weighed up my options. I had agreed to the pact, I had made the decision to find The One, and I'd gone on the three dates with three different guys, just as I'd said I would. Objectively, the date with Coleman had been great, but I could not get past the whole mortician slash dead bodies slash "I carve coffins for fun" thing with him.

Then, there was Nash. We had got on so well, and he seemed like a great guy, but there was that dog slobber situation I found incredibly off-putting, and I doubted I could ever kiss him without thinking about it.

And finally, Blaze. Nice guy, easygoing, possibly a sandwich or two short of a picnic, but possibly the best of the lot.

Three different guys, three different reasons not to date any one of them.

I turned back and looked at the sea of eager faces around the table, awaiting my verdict. Both Paige and Bailey were here with Cassie and me, having left their barista, Sophie, to "woman" the café counter, as they had put it.

"None of them." I closed my eyes, expecting the worst from my friends.

"What?!"

"Why?!"

"But they all seemed so good!"

"Are you crazy?"

A quieter voice said, "Well, *that* doesn't surprise me."

I snapped my eyes open to look at Cassie. "What did you say?"

She was sitting back in her chair, looking squarely at me. "I said, that doesn't surprise me."

I pressed my lips together. I didn't want to hear it, but I knew Cassie was right. By deciding not to see any of these guys again, I wasn't surprising my friends in the least. I was doing precisely what they would be expecting of me: a swift cut and run, no turning back.

I hung my head. "I wanted it to be different this time."

Paige, the sweetest one of us, reached across the table and placed her hand on my arm. "We know you did, honey."

"What was wrong with these ones, then?" Cassie asked, her voice deflated, as though I had let *her* down. Which, I guess, I had.

I sighed.

"How about you start at the top?" Bailey suggested. "Tell us what went wrong with each date, and we might be able to help you."

Cassie harrumphed. I shot her a withering look. "Not helping."

She leaned forward in her chair, her features softened. "I'm sorry. It's just . . . we'd all hoped you would find him, that's all."

I nodded. *Me too.*

"So, Coleman. What was the deal with him?" Bailey prompted.

"Coleman's a mortician," I stated glumly, thinking of him standing next to his coffin.

"And?" Bailey led.

"And . . . he's a *mortician*."

Bailey scrunched up her face. "I'm confused here. You knew that before you went on a date with him."

37

I widened my eyes. "Yeah, but I didn't *know* know it, you know?"

"I can see that," Cassie said, cutting off another forkful of her raspberry and chocolate cake. "That would totally creep me out, too."

"What happened with him?" Paige asked.

As everyone ate their respective cakes, I told my friends how the brunch date with Coleman had gone well—my mind doing overtime on Coleman's profession aside—and then how we had gone to his funeral parlor. I thought of Coleman's coffin. "The thing is, it was really beautiful. He's obviously very talented and has a great eye. It's just . . ." I shuddered.

Cassie chuckled. "You know what? If we rule the flirty mortician out, I won't lose any sleep over it," she said to Bailey and Paige, who both nodded their assent.

"What are you talking about, 'rule him out'? He's already gone, dead in the water, over," I replied, a little confused.

"Well," Bailey began cautiously, her eyes darting from Paige, to Cassie, and back to me. "You know how we decided Josh was perfect for Paige, even though she didn't think so at the time?"

"Yeah, how wrong was I?" Paige said with a grin.

Concerned I knew *exactly* where this was going, I replied, "Yes, but this is an entirely different situation. Paige agreed to us finding her a guy: *I* haven't done that." I furrowed my brow, my eyes shooting between my friends.

"True," Paige said with a nod, her head cocked to the side. "But, you said you wanted to find The One, and you went on these three Last First Dates."

"And you did agree to the pact. Both times," Cassie added with a wry smile.

"So?" I shook my head.

"So, we've agreed you need to give one of these guys a second chance," Paige said.

"You've 'agreed' this?" I was incredulous.

"That's right, and we're not taking 'no' for an answer," Cassie added, crossing her arms in that "don't mess with me" way I knew from work. She might have been one of my best friends, but she was also my boss.

"But . . . but . . ." I protested, doing my best fish impersonation as I tried to think of how to get out of what was rapidly becoming a dating intervention—not the friendly catch-up with my besties I'd anticipated.

"We think we need to help you push through this fussiness thing you've got going on, Marissa. That's why we want you to decide which one you're going to date and go on another date with him," Bailey said.

"With an open mind, of course," Cassie added, and Bailey and Paige both nodded their agreement.

"It's the only way," Paige said.

I blinked at my friends. "And you all agree?"

"Yes," they said in unison, nodding, like a group of Muppets—well-meaning but misguided Muppets, that was.

I pushed my plate away, my appetite gone. I bit my lip. "And you won't accept that I just test ran these guys and not one of them was right for me?"

"Nope," Cassie said as the others shook their heads in agreement. "But, you can rule out Mr. Mortician, if you like. We're good with that."

I thought about Coleman. Yes, ruling him out was a must. I literally *ran* away from him, after all. I'm not sure a girl can come back from that sort of thing.

At least the other dates weren't quite as . . . horrible.

"That leaves Nash and Blaze," Cassie said.

I thought about the two remaining guys. My date with Nash had been great, right up until that possible dog slobber transference situation at the end, that was. The thought of Dexter's saliva mingled with Nash's and mine still made me want to hurl. I moved on to Blaze. He may be "thick, strong, and thirsty," but he was a nice guy, extremely hot, and we'd had fun on our date, albeit with a little too much talk about working out and "improving" my body.

"Okay. If I have to do this—and I want you all to know I'm doing this under duress—I'll go on another date with . . ." I paused for dramatic effect, like they do on TV. ". . . Blaze."

We would get married, have good-looking little bodybuilders, and live happily ever after. Although, with the milk we'd go through, we may need to invest in a cow.

"Oh, yay! He is so cute!" Paige exclaimed.

"Dammit! My money was on Nash," Cassie exclaimed.

"What? You *bet* on this?" I asked, incredulous my friends would do something like that to me.

"There may have been a small wager placed," Cassie said with a small shrug, looking embarrassed. I watched as she reached into her purse, pulled out a twenty-dollar bill, and handed it to Paige. I then watched as Bailey did the same.

"Thank you very much," Paige said, folding the bills and slipping them into her own purse.

I regarded my friends, openmouthed. "You guys!"

"We wanted to make this interesting," Cassie said unapologetically.

"Spying on me going on three dates in one day wasn't interesting enough for you?" I asked, my eyebrows raised in question.

My friends merely grinned back at me. Clearly, it was not.

"All bets aside, I'm surprised you're going with Blaze," Cassie said.

"You're just bitter you backed the wrong horse, Cassie," Paige replied with a smug smile.

Cassie furrowed her brow. "No, it's more than that." She looked at me as she sunk her fork absentmindedly into what remained of her cake. "I'm curious, what did you two find to talk about on your date?"

"Oh, lots of stuff. Music, what we like to do in the weekends, what we drink . . ." I searched my brain for more.

"Working out?" Cassie asked, playing with her fork.

"Yeah, there was a bit of that." I twisted my empty coffee cup in its saucer.

No, there was a *lot* of that. My mind began to whirr, whipping me into a frenzy about how little Blaze and I had in common, how boring the whole bodybuilding thing was to me, and how little interest I had in eggy milk smoothies. *Ugh.*

Blaze may be as hot as an Arizona summer, but you couldn't base a relationship on that. Could you?

"You're not sure about him now, are you?" Cassie asked, examining my expression.

"No!" My tummy began to churn. "What am I going to do? I don't want to spend all my time at a gym, staring at my reflection in the mirror as I lift weights. And I do not want to drink a tuna smoothie, even if Blaze said they taste okay. Uh-ah, no way."

Bailey pulled a face. "Why would anyone want to drink a tuna smoothie?"

"Exactly!" I replied. I shook my head, chewing the inside of my lip. "No, it can't be Blaze. It just can't."

"That leaves Nash," Cassie said.

"What was the problem with him? He seemed really good on paper. He was the one who was all manly and defended you at the construction site, right?" Bailey asked.

"Yes," I replied begrudgingly, thinking of how dashing and sexy Nash had been that day. I let out a sigh. If it hadn't been for the dog-slobber situation, he would easily have been the front-runner.

"So, what happened? Everything looked good from our vantage point, right, Bailey?" Paige said, and Bailey agreed.

I picked up my fork and pushed my cake crumbs around my plate. Without looking up, I said, "If I tell you guys, will you promise not to judge me?"

There was a chorus of "sure" and "yes" from my friends.

"Well, you see, everything had gone really well, you know? He's a nice guy, maybe a little too into dogs, but we'd had fun. And I was thinking he might be The One, and then . . . well . . ." I paused as I struggled with how to say it. In the end, I simply blurted it out. "He let his dog lick his mouth, and then he kissed me."

"Euw!" All three of them said, recoiling from me in horror—just as I had from Nash.

"Inside his mouth?" Paige asked, her own mouth dropped open in obvious repulsion.

"No. It sort of skimmed the outside of his lips, I guess."

Cassie raised her eyebrows at me. "*Skimmed?*"

I shifted my weight in my seat. "Maybe? It was hard to tell."

She threw her hands up in the air. "Oh, my gosh, Marissa! You've totally overreacted to this. You've freaked out over virtually nothing!"

I crossed my arms, knitting my brows together. "No, the dog *did* lick his face, and then he *did* kiss me."

"There is a world of difference between a dog licking someone's face and a dog licking someone's mouth," Cassie replied, shooting me an "are you insane" look.

I glared back at her, pushing away the uncomfortable feeling inside that she may—just *may*—be right.

"You know, Marissa?" Bailey said, breaking our staring competition. "All you have to do is ask him not to let his dog lick his face while you're around."

"I guess."

I weighed up my options: I could either spend the next date, or ten, being asked to punch and squeeze and prod Blaze's various muscle groups, or I could simply do as Bailey suggested and ask Nash not to let Dexter lick his face if kissing was ever on the table.

In the end, there wasn't much of a competition.

I let out a heavy sigh, pressing my lips together. "All right. I guess I can do that."

"So, you'll go on a second date with Nash?" Cassie asked, her face lighting up.

"I'll go on another date with Nash"—I smiled at my friends, hoping like crazy I'd just made the right call—"*without* his dog."

"And you won't go making up problems out of nothing as an excuse not to date him?" Cassie asked, looking at me like a stern parent.

I pursed my lips. Begrudgingly, I admitted to myself I may have done that with the dog-slobber thing. I nodded.

"Awesome!" Cassie said with a glint in her eye.

I watched, slack-jawed, as she put her hand out and Paige fished around in her purse for the money. "Thank you, ladies," she said to them both as Paige handed over their money.

42

"You have *got* to be kidding me," I muttered.

"A bet's a bet," Bailey said with a shrug.

"It's not about the money. I really think you've made the right call in choosing Nash," Cassie said, pocketing her cash. "That creepy mortician guy and Mr. Muscles weren't for you."

I drummed my fingers on the table. *Nash.* I was going on a second date with Nash, a Last Second Date. Despite my persistent repulsion at the whole Dexter-saliva thing, a couple of butterflies beat their wings in my belly.

Maybe Nash would end up being the guy for me?

CHAPTER 5

J sat, waiting at Alessandro's Café, pushing my hair behind my ears several times, eyeing the entranceway. I had two lattes in front of me, remembering Nash had ordered one on our date last weekend. I had hoped it may soften him toward me after that whole botched-kiss thing the last time I saw him.

I had texted both Blaze and Coleman, thanking them for the dates and telling them I had decided not to see them again. I said I hoped there were no hard feelings, although in Coleman's case, I imagine he already had a voodoo doll of me with a fully sharpened pack of pins at the ready.

Blaze had texted me back, telling me I could work out with him whenever I wanted, but Coleman had gone into total radio silence. I could hardly blame him after what I'd done. I was ashamed, just thinking about it.

To meet Nash, I had purposefully chosen a canine-free location. Not that I had anything against Dexter. He was a great dog, I just wasn't so keen on being reminded of the dog-slobber situation that had caused this furor in the first place.

Although Nash had clearly been reluctant to meet me, I told him I needed to explain something. Of course, I had no intention of telling him the actual truth about why I ended our date so abruptly. What would have been the point in that? Instead, I'd made up a story about receiving an urgent, worrying message that had caused me to have to leave suddenly. It seemed convincing enough to me, and I hoped he'd buy it so we could move on.

Finally, a good eleven minutes late—I mean, how rude!—those hamsters turned up in my belly and began scuttling around again the moment I spotted Nash walk through the café door. He was wearing the same work combo of shorts, T-shirt, and work boots he was in the day I met him. Only this time, when his eyes landed on me, he wasn't smiling.

As he approached our table, I stood up to greet him, a smile placed firmly on my face. I had deliberated for hours over what to wear, not knowing what an "I'm sorry for getting freaked out over the dog saliva and would you like to go on another date with me" outfit looked like. In the end, I'd settled on my favorite navy pencil skirt, a cute pale pink blouse, and a pair of heels—it was a work day, after all.

"Hi, Nash. You look great." I beamed at him, trying my best to ignore the growing tension in my head.

"Thanks," he replied. Still no smile.

Without me inviting him, he sat down in the chair opposite me. I sat slowly down in my own chair, pushing my hair behind my ear once more, despite the fact it was very firmly there already.

It's going to be like that, is it?

After an awkward moment, during which Nash simply looked at me as though he was taking my measure, he said, "I was surprised to hear from you."

"Really?" I squeaked. "I had a great time on our date."

He cocked an eyebrow. "You did?"

"Oh, yes. You're great, Dexter's great, the restaurant was great. It was all . . ." I searched my mind for the correct word.

"Great?" Nash offered.

"Exactly. Great."

"Ah-huh," he said, clasping his hands together on the table. "So, how about the end of the date? Was that 'great' too?"

45

I shot him a puzzled look, pretending I didn't know what he was referring to: Dog Slobbergate.

"The kiss." His voice was low, quiet—pretty darn sexy, under different circumstances, actually.

I cleared my throat, distinctly uncomfortable. He was being very direct. "Ah, yes. That." I averted my eyes as my cheeks began to heat up.

"What was it? Technique? Attraction? Had you friend zoned me or something? But then, if you'd done that, you wouldn't have asked me on a second date, right?" He furrowed his brow. "Would you?"

I let out a puff of air. "Look, the thing is, I had a message that was very worrying and I had to leave, quickly. It had nothing to do with you, or Dexter, or anything." I let out a breath I hadn't known I was holding.

"With Dexter?" he questioned, looking more confused than he was before.

"Yes! It was nothing to do with Dexter." My voice had become unnaturally high. Why had I mentioned Dexter? I didn't need to, I hadn't rehearsed it. Mentioning Dexter just raised questions in Nash's mind, questions I didn't want to have to answer.

"Look, if you don't like my dog, then we're done here." He pushed his chair out from the table with a screech when the chrome of the chair scraped across the polished tiled floor. He straightened up, ready to leave.

"Nash, don't go! Please. I'll, I'll tell you the truth."

Without sitting, he replied, "All right."

"Please sit down. Please."

He studied my face for a moment before, thankfully, plunking himself back down on the chair.

My smile denied the nerves rattling around inside me.

"Shoot," he instructed.

I swallowed. "Well, here's the thing. I . . . I was a little put off by the . . ."

"The what?"

I scrunched up my face. "By the dog saliva." I looked up into his eyes, nervously awaiting his response.

He let out a short, sharp laugh. "The dog saliva?" He shook his head, leaning in toward me. "Marissa, what are you talking about?"

"Well, you may not remember this, but Dexter licked you on the lips just before you kissed me, and it . . . it kind of bothered me."

I watched as he leaned back in his chair, roaring with laughter. My eyes darted around the room as people at nearby tables turned to look at us. I smiled at them, hoping Nash's amusement would abate.

Eventually, after what felt like a long time, he rested his chin on his fist. "That's why you didn't want to kiss me, because you thought Dex had licked my lips?"

I gave him a weak nod. "I thought maybe it might have worked its way into your mouth, too."

He shook his head, a fresh smile teasing the edges of his mouth. "Marissa, Dex didn't lick my lips, and his saliva didn't get anywhere near my mouth. Granted, he licked my face, but that was an accident that sometimes happens with dogs, especially ones as affectionate as Dex."

"Are you sure he didn't get them? Not even the edge or something?"

"Marissa, I don't know what sort of guys you've dated in the past, but I'm not in the habit of French kissing dogs." He shook his head, chuckling to himself. "Hand on heart." He placed his hand on his chest and shot me a serious look—well, as serious as he could right now.

I almost sighed. He was more like Jon Snow than ever before. I could half imagine him in black robes, a manly scowl on his face as he plotted how to save The North from the Night Walkers. I sighed.

When I didn't respond immediately, Nash's eyebrow shot up again in question.

"All right, I can accept that. You didn't have any dog slobber on your mouth." I returned his smile, my anxiety receding.

"You had a little freak-out there, didn't you?"

I nodded, embarrassed.

"Do you do that a lot?"

"No, of course not," I replied, indignant.

He narrowed his eyes. "That's a lie, isn't it?"

"No?" I chanced.

He shook his head, chuckling. He reached across the table and found my hand. Holding it in his, he said in a low voice, "I like you, Marissa." I nodded, my mouth suddenly dry. "How about you tell me the next time something bothers you and we'll deal with it?"

There was going to be a next time? Those hamsters started up a tap-dancing routine in my belly. "Okay."

"Good." He still held my hand in his, and I liked the feeling. It was a strong, warm hand, the kind of hand you could rely on. "In that case, would you mind if we tried it again?"

"Tried what again?"

"This." He put his fingers under my chin and gently lifted my face so we were looking into one another's eyes. I swallowed down a lump in my throat. He leaned over the small table and gently brushed his lips against mine, right there and then, in the café, in front of everyone.

And I didn't care, not one little bit.

And you know why? It felt good. No, scratch that, it felt *amazing*. He slipped his hand around the back of my head, and I breathed in his scent. I was lost in our kiss, the world around me a blur of voices and music and unidentifiable sounds, merging into nothing.

He pulled away from me, his eyes dancing. "Better?"

I swear, I saw stars.

"Better," I confirmed breathlessly, while inside my brain yelled "Best kiss ever!" and my toes curled in my shoes.

He nodded at me, sitting back in his chair. "Good. I assume that means the freak-out is over?"

I bit back a smile. "Oh, yes."

He let out a soft laugh. If I'd known Nash could kiss like that, I don't think I would have freaked out in the first place. Okay, maybe I would have, but I wouldn't have wanted to.

"Is that for me?" he asked, gesturing at the cups of coffee on the table.

"Oh, yes! I'd totally forgotten. I got you a latte."

He picked the cup up and took a sip. "Mm, cold coffee. My favorite."

We grinned at one another, enjoying our rediscovered closeness.

He finished his coffee in a couple of short gulps and placed the cup back on the saucer. "So, now we've got that sorted out, I know you work at AGD, but what exactly do you do that means you get to dress up like Miss Moneypenny for work?"

My cheeks heated up. "I'm an account manager."

"Oh. Is that like being an accountant?"

I shook my head. "No, I'm in sales. I sell telecommunications solutions to businesses. I've been doing it for a while, and I really like it."

"That's impressive," he replied with a smile as the heat continued to rise in my cheeks. "I'm glad you're not an accountant. Aren't they boring as hell?"

I laughed. "I don't know."

"I don't, either, but I've totally bought into the whole urban myth about dull accountants, so it's just as well you're in sales, instead."

"Just as well." I smiled at him, as something moved in my chest.

This is good, this is very good.

My phone buzzed insistently on the table between us. "Sorry," I muttered as I flipped it over. I read the reminder, telling me I had a team meeting back at the office in ten minutes. *Dammit!* That's what you got for making dates in the middle of the work day.

"I've got to go," I said, wishing I didn't have to.

"That's too bad. I'll walk you out."

We wandered out of the café and out onto the street where we stopped and turned to face one another.

"I'm really pleased you called," Nash said, smiling down at me and taking my hand in his.

"Me too. Thanks for . . . not thinking I'm crazy."

He laughed. "Oh, I didn't say *that*."

I whacked him playfully on the arm. "Well, then." I looked up into his blue eyes.

"Well, then," he echoed, gazing so intently at me, my heart rate kicked up about a gazillion notches.

He slipped his free hand up my arm and onto my shoulder. "You know how we did that thing in there, the thing you seemed to like?"

I nodded, my throat turning dry.

"If it's okay with you, I'd like to do it some more. A lot more."

"Me too."

And then he leaned down and did it again, he kissed my socks off. Well, not that I was wearing any socks, because on a grown woman in corporate clothes, that would just look weird. But if I were wearing any socks, they would have been well and truly kissed off me by this gorgeous man, right there on the sidewalk.

"Can I see you this weekend?" he asked.

"That would be nice."

"I'll text you."

With great reluctance, I tore myself away from him, turned and walked down the street. My heart felt like it could burst right out of my chest. I had made the right decision. Nash was the man for me. He liked me and accepted me for my crazy freak-out ways.

And oh, my! What a kisser!

Perhaps he was The One after all? Perhaps this was going to work? Perhaps this had been my Last Second Date?

CHAPTER 6

I returned to the office, floating on a cloud of happiness, my feet barely touching the floor. Nash liked me, and I liked him back. No freak-outs, no bolting from the scene of the date, just a cup of (cold) coffee and some outstanding kissing with a very, very hot guy.

I let out a contented sigh. *This must be what it's like for normal people.*

I dropped my purse at my desk and headed straight to Cassie's office. Cassie had become Regional Sales Manager a few short months ago and got her own office with a view of the city with a sliver of a glimpse of Auckland's beautiful harbor. Although she was my boss, it hadn't affected our friendship. I was a hard worker—when I wasn't meeting hot men at cafés in the middle of the work day, that was—and always delivered great results. In fact, since Cassie had been promoted, I had taken her place as one of the top selling account managers in the team, a record I was extremely proud of.

"Knock, knock," I said, leaning up against the door frame, peering in at Cassie, hard at work on her computer.

Cassie's head bobbed up, and her look of concentration transformed into a grin. "Come in, close the door. I take it you have news?" She stood up and walked around her desk toward the comfortable chairs she had arranged around a small, wooden table by the large window.

Closing the door behind me, my tummy performed a fresh flip-flop at the thought of Nash. "I do." It would have taken superhuman strength to suppress the grin that wanted to spread across my face, a strength I didn't possess today.

I sat down and crossed my legs. Looking at Cassie's face, upturned in anticipation, my heart expanded. "It was good, really good."

"And he was okay with the whole dog thing and your freak-out?"

I nodded. "He was. In fact, he said Dexter's—that's his dog's name, which is really cool, isn't it?" I sidetracked myself, thinking of how cute Nash and Dexter were together, adding to Nash's charm. Why I had decided to choose Blaze over Nash was utterly beyond me right now. "Anyway, he said his dog's lick didn't even come near his lips and that he doesn't usually let him lick his face. So, we're all good."

Cassie shook her head, smiling. "You are so funny, Marissa. But I'm happy for you."

I beamed. "Thanks. I am too."

"So, you're seeing him again?"

"Of course! We're going out on Saturday."

"Oh, that's so exciting. Your third date."

"I really want it to work out. Nash even said he would help me through my next freak-out."

Cassie raised her eyebrows. "He did? Wow, he sounds amazing."

"I know, right? Amazing."

Cassie grinned at me. "I have a feeling about you."

I had a feeling about us, too. "It's got to work," I added solemnly.

Cassie narrowed her eyes at me. "Because of the pact?"

"Yes, that's right: the pact." A knot tightened in my belly. Since we had first agreed to the pact to marry the next guy we dated, I hadn't exactly taken it as seriously as the others.

But now, things had changed.

Cassie raised her eyebrows in question, her eyes trained on me. She had the ability to say everything without saying a single word, and it was making me very uncomfortable.

I swallowed, not wanting to have this conversation right now—or at any time, if I was completely honest. I shrugged. "And I . . . I want what you have with Will," I added, hoping to deflect her attention.

"Uh-huh," she replied, her eyes searching my face. *Dammit!* She wasn't deflected in the least!

I squirmed uncomfortably in my seat. I needed a change of subject, stat!

"So, I'm seeing Pukeko Chocolates today, to pitch a solution. Want me to try and nab some of that earl grey tea–flavored chocolate you like?"

"Hang on. Let's get back to this 'it's got to work' thing."

I'd pulled out the big guns, and failed. I had felt sure if anything could distract my sweet-toothed friend from her line of questioning it would be chocolate.

I scrunched up my face. "Do we have to?"

"Why does it 'have to work'? What's going on, Marissa? What are you not telling me?" Cassie's voice was filled with suspicion—and concern.

I hated to admit it, but I crumbled. Man, I would make a terrible spy if I was captured and interrogated by the enemy.

I let out a sigh. "It's my ex, Eddie. We dated a long time ago. He . . . he got engaged." I hung my head.

Cassie's mouth formed a perfect "o" but no words came out.

"It's not that I'm trying to say 'well, look at me, I'm in a relationship, too' or anything, you understand, it's just that it made me realize it was about time I got serious about getting serious with a guy, and the pact seemed like the perfect way to do it, and . . . well, here I am, dating Nash," I said, rapid-fire.

Cassie raised her eyebrows. "Are you sure? I mean, it can be a big thing when an ex gets engaged. It can bring up all sorts of things."

"No! It's nothing like that. It's so much more nuanced."

Nuanced my ass. Eddie had been my Big Love, the guy I fell for hard. We were together for three years, and I had thought we would last forever. And then he broke up with me, out of the blue. It was like a hurricane blasting through my life, devastating me. It took a long, long time to get over Eddie Sutcliffe.

"Is it really, Marissa? Are you sure you're not having a knee-jerk reaction to this guy becoming engaged?"

Again, I crumbled. And again, I would make a terrible spy. "Maybe a little bit? Or a whole lot? One or the other, I haven't decided yet." I pouted.

I remembered Eddie's smile, the way he made me feel so special, something I had never had before. He quickly became the center of my world, and life without him was unimaginable.

Until I had to.

Cassie shook her head. "Oh, Marissa."

I put my hands up in surrender. "It's okay. Everything's good. I admit, I may have decided to find The One because of the whole Eddie marrying a perfect-looking ice queen thing, but I genuinely like Nash, *really*, I do."

"Okay. So, what's the deal with this Eddie guy? When did you two date?"

"We met in my last year in college and dated for a few years. He was my first."

"The first guy you slept with?"

"Yes, and . . . my first boyfriend."

"Wow, a late bloomer."

"Something like that."

None of my friends knew about my teenage confidence and weight issues, and I had zero interest in sharing now. It wasn't long after I'd lost the weight and begun to feel better about myself when I had met Eddie. We hit it off immediately, and I was genuinely surprised when he asked me out. I hadn't gotten used to the idea guys would find me attractive, I'd been invisible to them for so long. We started dating and, for the first time in my life, the pieces had felt like they had fallen into place. And that's the way it was for three years, two months, and seventeen days. Until he broke my heart.

Cassie's phone beeped on her desk. She stood up. "I had better get back to work."

"Sure." I couldn't help but feel as though I'd let her down, like she could no longer trust my intentions. Or maybe it was me I was letting down, me I couldn't trust? I pushed the unsettling thoughts from my mind.

Cassie turned to me as I reached for the door handle. "You know what? I hope you are genuine about your feelings for Nash and you're not just hankering after something you can't have."

"Please trust me?" My voice was almost pleading.

"It wouldn't be fair to mess Nash around, you know. Not if you're still in love with your ex."

I let out a startled laugh. Still in love with Eddie? Was she *insane?* "No way. It's all good."

I thought of Nash, sitting across from the table at Alessandro's, smiling at me, and I knew what I had begun to feel for him was real. It was special, and it was genuine—whether or not I had something to prove to Eddie Sutcliffe.

* * *

I REACHED my desk and plunked myself down in my chair, staring absentmindedly at the cute puppies calendar I had on my cubicle wall. Despite the churning in my belly, a small smile spread across my face. I should tell Nash I had pictures of dogs at work. He'd like that.

"Hi, Marissa, is it?" a voice said.

I swung around in my chair and came face-to-face with the newest member of the sales team.

"Yes, it is. Hi, Antoinette." I nearly chuckled. This girl wasn't French, so what kind of name was that? A pretentious one, that's what it was.

"I wondered if you could help me? I don't know how to work the printer."

Antoinette Smith—You see? Unless I'd missed something, Smith was *so* not a French name—had joined AGD on Monday, and already half the guys in the team were in love with her. Well, probably in *lust* with her, you know how men could be. With her long blond hair, her short, tight dresses, and more makeup than a drag queen on debut, she definitely fell into the "sex siren" category in that obvious way men can't help but lap up.

When we had first met, I'd found it hard to take her seriously. She looked like she belonged on the set of the *Baywatch* movie, not in a telecommunications sales team. Cassie had told me confidentially that she had been forced to employ Antoinette as she was her boss's niece. Nepotism was alive and well at AGD, it would seem.

I hopped out of my seat, glad of the distraction from my love life. Antoinette may not be my type of person, but that didn't mean I couldn't be nice. "Sure, no problem."

I walked with her through the sales office, noticing the male team members' eyes following us, their tongues virtually hanging out, as we made our way to the photocopy room. I rolled my eyes. *Men.* Subtlety was not their forte. I glanced at Antoinette. She seemed to lap the attention up, walking like Marilyn Monroe, her hips swinging from side to side.

"Okay, what are you trying to do?" I asked as we stood facing the printer.

"I sent something to print, but it hasn't turned up here."

"It might be in one of these." I leaned down and checked the trays running along the side of the behemoth machine. Why it needed so many trays was beyond my understanding. I found a couple of loose pieces of paper and pulled them out. "Is this what you're looking for?"

"Oh, yes!" Antoinette replied, her face lighting up as though she were a child and I'd just announced she was going to Disneyland. "Thank you so much."

I handed the paper over to her and said, "Next time, choose tray seven. For some reason, that's the main tray."

"I will," she replied with a nod, her face serious.

Back at my desk, I pulled up my action list and set about ticking items off before our team catch-up at eleven. I put the final touches on the presentation I planned to give Pukeko Chocolates this afternoon, and I ran through precisely what I was going to say in my head, mouthing the words out as I looked at my screen.

Eleven o'clock rolled around and I accompanied the rest of the team into the boardroom where we took our seats around the large oak table. I watched with amusement as a couple of my male colleagues fussed over Antoinette, pulling a chair out for her, offering her water—generally making idiots of themselves. She took it all in her stride, smiling and simpering at them like a fifties movie star. I bet she got it all day, every day.

"Right, everyone. Let's get down to it," Cassie said, standing at the front of the room in front of a large, empty screen. She clicked a key on her laptop, and a diagram appeared on the screen behind her.

I had to pull my glasses out of their case and give them a wipe to see the screen.

"As you can see on this chart, we had a good, solid quarter," Cassie began.

The chart showed a small rise in profit, but an equally small rise in costs.

"I'm not going to beat about the bush here, guys. We need a better quarter, starting from right now." She sat down at the table. "Let's hear your top projections. Marissa? Why don't you kick things off for us?"

I glanced down at the spreadsheet I had printed off prior to my coffee with Nash this morning. I had the name of each of my customers in one column, their current revenue, projected increases based on my upcoming pitches, and my estimated percentage success rate. I was prepared.

"No problem. First up, I have a data solution I'm pitching to Pukeko Chocolates this afternoon with Bryce." I smiled across the room at the technology specialist I often worked with. He was the absolute best. "Even though this is only my third appointment with them, I'm pretty confident they have short-listed us and Telco, and I plan on blowing them out of the water with our new voice-data-connectivity solution. I've placed that at a seventy-five percent likelihood."

"Excellent. We've never had their business and it's big, so anything you need from the team, you let me know." I nodded. "What's the projected revenue?"

I gave Cassie my figures and watched as she typed them into her laptop. I had been working on Pukeko Chocolates for weeks, having followed up on a lead from our telephone support team, and I was *this* close to winning their business, I could feel it in my bones. Winning it would be a major coup for me, plus it would set me up nicely to achieve my annual target, which, I hoped, could lead to a promotion to Account Director within the team. *Marissa Jones, Account Director.* I liked the sound of that.

Today was my final push, and I was hoping, with Bryce's expertise and my savvy, we would put this one to bed very soon.

Cassie continued to go around the room, asking for each team member's predictions. I watched her work quickly and efficiently, asking pertinent questions and offering support or advice where needed. When it came to Antoinette's turn, all eyes were on her. She sat in her seat, her cleavage pushing its way out of her tight top, toying with her long blond hair.

"Antoinette, as you're new here and haven't gotten to know your customers yet to be able to make any projections, maybe you'd like to tell us all a little bit about yourself? This is day two here for you?"

"Yes, it is, and I have to say, I love it here. You all have been so welcoming to me." She put her hand against her chest, and I could have sworn many eyes nearly popped out of their sockets as they watched the gesture. "All of you," she said, gesturing with her hands, "are awesome!"

As she flicked her arm out, her watch got caught in her long hair, pulling it out to the side so she looked like she was wearing some kind of wide hood made of hair. But, although her hand didn't stop, her hair did, pulling a large clump out of her head.

I sucked in air. *That had to hurt!*

I looked at the hair attached to the watch and noticed it was a hair extension. She'd pulled one of her hair extensions off her head. *How embarrassing for the poor girl!*

"Oops!" she cried, lowering her hand to hide it under the table. She

THREE LAST FIRST DATES

yanked desperately, eventually loosening the extension from the watch with a *thud* when her fist hit the underside of the oak table.

I caught her eye and mouthed, "Are you okay?" and she nodded back, clearly humiliated.

"Thank you, Antoinette," Cassie said, coming to her rescue. "We're glad you're here. I'd like you to shadow someone for the next few weeks to learn about our solutions and see how we interact with our customers."

"That sounds great," she simpered, her hair now successfully detached from her watch. Her head looked a little lopsided now.

"Kieran, Marissa, Jason, and Sally?" Cassie said, naming the most experienced members of the team. "Can one of you please take Antoinette to your meetings for the next few days? I'd like her to see you at work."

"I'd be happy to," Jason said immediately, almost before Cassie had finished speaking.

"Me, too. I've got loads on. You could watch how it's done," Kieran said eagerly.

I noticed Sally stayed quiet, echoing my own silence. Antoinette seemed sweet enough, but I had things going on right now and could do without the added responsibility.

"Thank you both so much, Kieran and Jason. You're both so wonderful to me, and I really appreciate all the help you've offered me since I joined."

She was being so sickly sweet, I could vomit.

She turned her attention to me. "I think I might go with Marissa, if that's okay with you?"

My eyes got huge. "Me?" I questioned. I glanced at Cassie. Her eyes gave her away, but her face was as calm and in control as always. "Would you be happy with that, Marissa?" she questioned.

I shrugged. "Sure, Antoinette. That's fine."

She beamed at me. "Thank you."

I may have to shove a few of my male customers' tongues back in their mouths when she walked through the door with me, but I was

59

certain I could manage that. What harm could it do to have her tag along?

* * *

No harm at all, as it turned out. That afternoon, I only had to do one tongue shove at the start of the meeting, and the others on the Pukeko team seemed impervious to her charms, much to my relief. I had a job to do and business to close; I didn't need any distractions.

As I stood at the front of the room with Bryce, wrapping up the reasons why choosing AGD Telecommunications over our rival was the best decision Pukeko Chocolates could make, they were utterly riveted.

I knew it had gone well. They had asked the right questions, and between Bryce and me, we answered them all, dispelling their concerns.

On the way back to the office, Antoinette peppered me with question after question about our pitch and the customer. She didn't let up, even once I was back at my desk.

She was eager, I'd give her that. Surprisingly so for someone who got her position because of a family member on the executive team.

"And that was why you decided to go with that particular solution?"

"It was. You see, I think it's always best to get to know a customer and their needs before you even get to pitching." I placed my laptop on my desk and plugged it in.

"Exactly," Antoinette said with a smile. She took my hand in hers, training her (unnaturally) blue eyes on mine. I wondered what her actual eye color was. "Marissa, thank you so much for this. I've learned so much from you."

"You're welcome, Antoinette."

Antoinette looked from one side to the other, then leaned down toward me. "Can I ask you a question?" she asked in a hushed tone.

"Sure."

"Do you think I'm right for this sort of place? I mean, a lot of people look at me funny."

"What do you mean?"

She screwed up her face. "I mean . . . the men."

"Oh." I tilted my chair back. "Yeah, I've noticed that." I would have to be blind not to have.

Her cheeks flushed a delicate shade of pink, and I instantly felt bad for her, despite the fact I knew she played the "damsel in distress" with the men in the office half the time. Really, she could single-handedly set the women's movement back a decade with the amount of eyelash fluttering and hip swinging this woman did around the office.

"What I mean is, I think a lot of the guys here think you're very attractive."

"Oh." She nodded, biting her lip. "Is it the way I dress?"

I pursed my lips and thought for a moment. Would Antoinette appreciate me suggesting she tone her look down, perhaps lose the hair extensions that seemed to have a life of their own? Maybe even go so far as to wear clothes in her *actual* size? I decided, yes. If I were new here and asked someone's advice, I would want to hear the truth.

I cleared my throat. "Look, Antoinette. Have you ever thought about maybe, I don't know, changing the way you dress?"

She stood up straight, pulling her hands defensively around her small waist. "What's wrong with the way I dress?"

I took in her loose hair, falling in soft curls to her elbows, her tight, low-cut, sleeveless top, her short black skirt, her sky-high heels. Really, she didn't look too dissimilar to a lady of the night. "I don't know, maybe cover up a bit? That way the guys won't gawp at you so much."

She nodded, slowly. "Okay. I might try that." Her face broke back into a smile. "Thanks, Marissa. You're a real friend."

I glowed. I'd gone from thinking Antoinette was some silly girl, riding on her aunt's coattails, to realizing she was just as insecure as the rest of us and trying to find her place in the world.

It was quite a turnaround.

"Now, I need to get back to my desk to write this all up. Can I grab you a coffee?"

I smiled at her. Perhaps I'd misjudged her? She was interested and keen to learn. Perhaps I'd been as bad as the guys on the team who treated her as nothing more than a sex symbol? "That would be great. Milk and no sugar, please."

"Coming right up!"

I sat down at my desk and pulled out my phone. A smile spread across my face as I noticed a text from Nash.

Just checking in. Hope no freak-outs occurring. If so, text immediately. xx

I held the phone against my chest for a moment, grinning like a Disney princess in love. Not only was Nash cute and funny and quite possibly the best kisser on the face of the planet, he signed his message with not one but *two* kisses. I fired off a quick message in response.

No freak-outs. Thanks for today.

I paused, my finger hovering over the keyboard, then added "xx" to the end, hastily pressing "send" before I had the chance to delete it. I waited, sitting at my desk, holding on to my phone like it was a lifeline. I didn't have to wait long for a reply.

Looking forward to Saturday. Pick you up at six?

I replied in the affirmative, texting him my address. I placed my phone back on my desk and let out a contented sigh. Eddie's engagement to that ice queen may have put me in a tailspin at the time, but now that I'd been on two dates with Nash, I knew in my heart I did want to find The One.

And I had a pretty strong feeling I had.

CHAPTER 7

*P*atience never being my strong suit, Saturday could not come around fast enough for me. I had put my head down and worked my buns off for the rest of the week, glad of the distraction. Antoinette had continued to shadow me, and we had been getting on nicely. My experience with her was a lesson for me to give people more of a chance in the future. She had even taken my advice and worn skirts for the rest of the week that almost met her knee—give or take three inches. It was baby steps, but that was better than nothing.

Once again, I had carefully planned my outfit for my date with Nash. This time there was no instruction to "wear sensible shoes," so I went a little wild with it and wore my favorite pair of pale pink strappy heels, teamed with a white slim-fitting skirt and a floaty, sleeveless blouse done up to the neck. I was a great follower of the "less is more" approach, erring on the side of classy, with perhaps a smattering of sexy.

A spritz of Calvin Klein and one final check in my bedroom mirror and I collected my purse from the end of my bed, ready for my date. I went out into the living room where Ryan was almost prostrate on the sofa, watching a rugby match on TV, a beer in his hand.

KATE O'KEEFFE

I surveyed the room, my formerly gorgeous living room, with its soft white sofas, hardwood floors, and exposed brick walls—fake, of course, Auckland was on a major fault line—now littered with empty packets of chips, takeaway boxes, and Ryan's discarded clothes. It even smelled of boy.

"What are you up to tonight?" I asked him with a wrinkled nose as I plumped the cushions on the sofa he wasn't currently lazing on. *And when are you moving out?*

"Not much," he harrumphed, not taking his eyes from the screen.

"Well, whatever you do, have fun. I'm off out."

He turned his head slowly to look at me, raising his eyebrows when he saw my serious date ensemble. "Going somewhere fancy?"

"Actually, I have no idea where I'm going. Nash is picking me up in a few minutes. I figured, since it's almost six, we'll be going for drinks and dinner."

He pushed himself up from his spot on the sofa onto his elbows. "Isn't this the guy who took you to a *dog park* for your first date? You might want to grab a pair of rubber boots on your way out the door."

"Oh, very funny, brother. He didn't say anything about sensible shoes this time, so I can't imagine it will be a dog park," I replied with significantly more confidence than I felt. I glanced down at my white skirt and strappy, completely impractical shoes.

"Yeah, well, whatever you do tonight, you know it's all doomed, right? You'll end up a sad old sack, just like your brother here." He took a slug of his beer and returned his attention to the TV.

My brother, the positivity coach.

Truth be told, he hadn't always been like this. In fact, up until his ex, Amelia, dumped him, he'd been . . . normal. Now, all he did was mope around my apartment, eat junk, drink beer, *not* shave—or, I suspected, wash—and watch TV. I hoped it was a short-lived phase for his sake, and because I wanted my living room back.

Right on cue, the buzzer sounded.

Nash.

"I'm coming down," I said into the speaker. The last thing I wanted was for Nash to meet my "oh, woe is me" brother. *He* might have a

64

freak-out, and there could only be one person in a relationship who did that.

I said goodbye to Ryan, who grunted something about inevitable heartbreak to me without budging from his spot on the sofa, and sashayed down the stairs and out onto the street. I was greeted by Nash, standing on the sidewalk in front of a white pickup truck with "Campbell Construction" emblazoned on the side. He was wearing jeans, a light blue dress shirt with the sleeves rolled up, showing off his tanned, toned arms, and a smile that could light the entire street.

"Hey, you," he said with a grin that was impossible to resist. I stepped into him, and he slid his arms around my waist, planting one of his miraculous kisses on my lips.

"Hey," I responded, stars dancing in front of my eyes.

If this happened every time we kissed, I was going to turn into an astronaut.

"You look amazing, by the way."

I beamed at him. "Thanks. Not so bad yourself." I glanced down at his jeans. This was the first time I'd seen him in something other than a pair of shorts. He looked somehow more grown up, but just as hot—perhaps even more so.

I could barely believe I'd had second thoughts about this guy. He was . . . perfect.

"Shall we?" he asked.

"I think we shall."

He opened the passenger door for me to slide in, which I did as elegantly as I could in my slim-fitting skirt. He jumped in the other side and flashed me that knee-weakening grin as he turned the ignition.

"Where are we going?"

"I've got a date plan. You'll just have to wait and see. First stop is my place. I have something I want to show you."

A six-minute drive later, Nash pulled his truck into his driveway—the scene of our almost-kiss. I pushed the memory from my mind as best I could.

We got out of the car and walked to the front door.

"Ladies first," he said as he opened the glossy blue door.

"Thank you." I stepped over the threshold and into a long hallway with polished hardwood floors, and a single pendant light, hanging from the ceiling. The white walls were covered in framed photographs. A handful were of happy, perky dogs, and there was one of an older couple, smiling out at the camera. Nash's parents, I assumed. They weren't hung in any particular design, seemingly added to the collection as time went by. The overall effect was warm, inviting, just the way I'd always hoped these cottages would be.

"Prepare yourself," Nash said, his hand on the knob of a door to my right.

"What for?" I asked as he swung the door open, and I had my answer immediately as I was virtually bowled over by a pack of happy, lick-y, excited, squirmy puppies.

"The kids," Nash said way too late.

"Oh, my gosh. They are adorable!" I squealed, crouching down to pet them as they squirmed all over the floor at my feet, trying to climb onto my lap. They had black faces, trimmed with brown, their ears sticking up in the top of their soft, fluffy heads. "Yes, you are. You're adorable."

One of them managed to climb up onto my lap where it rolled on its back, ready for a tummy rub, which I gave willingly as the others continued to clamor for my attention at my feet.

I looked up at Nash who was smiling down at me. "These are your puppies?"

He chuckled. "If they're not, we've got a puppy house invasion on our hands."

I chuckled as I stood up, holding the one that had climbed up on my lap in my arms. "Don't they just melt your heart?"

"That they do," he replied, giving the pup's head a pat. "I thought you might like them."

"Like them? I *love* them," I gushed. "What breed are they?"

"Definitely part German Shepherd, because that's what mom is, but we're not sure what they're crossed with."

"Were they abandoned?" I asked, wondering how anyone in their right mind would want to desert such beautiful creatures.

Nash bent down and picked one of the puppies up off the floor. "Well, their mother was. She was picked up roaming the streets in West Auckland. She was in a fairly sorry state. But the pups are all healthy, and she's regaining her strength. Want to meet her?"

"Of course!" I replied, wondering how I had ever been freaked out by dog slobber.

"She's in here."

Still holding my puppy, who was now attempting to nibble off my earlobe—which was as ticklish as it sounded—I followed Nash into his living room. It wasn't a large room, but it was thoroughly charming. There was a beaten-up-looking brown leather sofa up against the wall and a couple of corduroy armchairs around a low, wooden coffee table. The sofa faced an open fireplace, which had a large grate in front of it, presumably to stop the puppies trying to become canine chimney sweeps on their adventures.

Curled up in a cane basket next to the sofa was a German Shepherd. She had to be the squirmy gang's mom. I looked over at her. Frankly, she looked exhausted, and I couldn't blame her: five puppies with the combined energy of an atomic bomb would be enough to tire out the best of them. When she spotted Nash, her tail began to bang furiously against the edge of the basket. She stood up to greet him and he patted her from the top of her head right down her back.

"Hey, Gretel," he said to her. "Gretel, this is my friend, Marissa."

Friend? I raised my eyebrows, a smile teasing the edges of my mouth. Friends didn't kiss like Nash and I did. Maybe he didn't want Gretel to know we were dating? Perhaps she was the jealous type?

I put the puppy carefully down on the ground and reached out to pat her. The tail kept wagging. "Hi there, Gretel." I looked at Nash. "How do you know her name?"

"We don't. But she looked like a Gretel, don't you think?" He smiled down affectionately at her. It suited him. In fact, it made him even more attractive. "I mean, she's a German Shepherd, so I needed a German name."

"And you'd read the story about the gingerbread house when you were a kid, right?"

He shrugged, chuckling. "It was either Gretel or Heidi Klum, and I figured she might be offended if I named a dog after her."

"I bet." I let out a laugh, enjoying the relaxed, easy feeling between us.

"Will you help me collect the puppies up?"

"Sure." We tracked the five puppies down—a harder task than you might think, even in a small living room—and Nash set up a pen around Gretel's bed. We placed the pups in with their mom, who lay down, looking exhausted once again.

"You hold tight. I'll go and get Dex. He'll be sad he's missing out on all the action."

Nash returned a moment later with Dexter, who bounded into the room and straight over to me, his tail wagging. I gave him a pat. "Dexter! How are you, boy?" I made a conscious effort to push the Slobber-gate freak-out from my mind.

"He likes you," Nash said, watching me as I patted Dexter.

"What's not to like?" I joked, smiling at him.

"That's a very good point."

I looked into his electric eyes. Those belly hamsters of mine whipped themselves into a frenzy. There was something about this guy, something . . . I struggled to put my finger on it. Whatever it was, it felt big, really big. And it didn't scare me.

Well, maybe a little.

"Dex is pretty happy to be in here. You see, he wasn't allowed near the pups until they were about a month old."

"Oh?"

"Male dogs can be aggressive toward puppies. But now?" He patted Dexter who gazed up at him adoringly. "Now, he's awesome. Okay. Would you like a drink before we head out?"

"Sure. A glass of wine?"

"I have red or white. Sorry, I'm not much of a wine connoisseur, even though I think the white may be a chardonnay?"

"A chardonnay would be perfect."

Nash disappeared out of the room. Dexter wandered over to the edge of the pen and sniffed at Gretel, who beat her tail in greeting once more. I reached into the pen and picked up one of the puppies and sat down on the sofa. I recognized it as the one I was holding before.

"Hello, you," I said as the puppy tried to lick my nose. For some reason, puppy slobber was an entirely different ballgame to me from dog slobber. I had no clue why. "Are you a girl? You look like you should be a girl." I held her up and checked. "Yes, you're a girl. Or at least, I think you are."

She had a line of light brown fur, running from between her eyes down to her nose. In my opinion, she was easily the most adorable of the lot—and the competition was stiff.

The puppy squirmed all over me as I patted her. I looked down at the state of my once-pristine white skirt, now covered in dog fur and the odd smear. I let out a sigh. So much for looking sophisticated tonight. I smiled to myself; I had a feeling Nash simply wouldn't care.

A moment later, he walked back into the room, holding a glass in one hand and a bottle of beer in the other. Taking in the current puppy situation, he placed my glass and his bottle on the coffee table in front of us.

"Let me help you out there," Nash said as he plucked the puppy off me and put her in the fenced pen next to the sofa with her mother and siblings. I watched them, mesmerized. They were so happy, so excited by, well, *everything*. I stole a glance at Nash as he sat down on the sofa next to me.

Kind of the way I felt right now.

He handed me my glass, and I looked down at it, puzzled.

"Sorry, I don't have any proper wine glasses."

I smiled at him. "No worries."

He held his beer bottle up. "Cheers."

We clinked glasses, and I settled into the sofa.

With his free hand, Nash took mine in his and began to play with my fingers. "You know, I was a little nervous about bringing you here."

"Why? You have a lovely place," I said, looking around the room.

There were floor-to-ceiling bookcases on either side of the fireplace, stacked with magazines, framed photos, and books, lots of books. Nash was a reader. Who knew? Every little thing I learned about him made him more and more my kind of guy.

"I didn't mean the house. I meant the dogs."

"I love dogs! Especially these ones. I mean, look at them."

He laughed. "Yeah, I can see that, which is awesome. But there was that whole dog-slobber issue before, and I thought maybe—"

I shushed him with my finger, wishing he hadn't mentioned it. "Let's not go there again, okay?" I darted a look at Dexter, lying at Nash's feet.

No, Marissa. Don't even think about it.

"Good idea."

"So, do I pass the test?" I asked, pushing any residual anxiety I had felt from my mind.

"Oh, yes." He grinned at me and took another sip of his beer. I followed suit, taking an extra-large gulp of my wine. I was absolutely determined not to let my fear of commitment get in the way, and freaking out again was a surefire way of ruining this date—and any chance with Nash.

"But, you know what?" Nash continued. "If you hadn't fallen for the dogs as you did, I don't think I could see you again."

"You couldn't?"

He shook his head. "It's a deal breaker for me. I'm a dog person." He shrugged. "Whoever I date needs to be, too."

"Well, I'm not sure I would describe myself as a 'dog person,'" I replied, doing air quotes, "but I really like dogs. My brother and I begged our parents for one for years. We finally got one, a crazy Soft Coated Wheaten Terrier, when I was about nine."

A broad grin spread across his face, and my breath caught in my throat. "You're a dog person."

I shrugged, holding his gaze. "I guess I am."

He leaned in toward me and brushed his lips against mine. It was just as magical as all our kisses had been, and any lingering fear I may freak out again disappeared in a flash.

Once he pulled away from me, he had the goofiest look on his face. My smile broadened. We both took another sip of our drinks.

"So, what are we doing after this?" I asked, loving the feeling of closeness I had to this guy—a guy I had run away from only two short dates ago.

"I thought, what better way to spend an evening with a beautiful woman than on a picnic at Mission Bay."

"A picnic?" I asked, taking a quick look down at my outfit, right down to my sky-high heels.

Nash followed my line of sight. "You can kick those off once we're there, sit back, and relax. And I've got some cushions to sit on, all packed up and ready to go."

I chuckled, shaking my head. "You've thought of everything."

Ten minutes and much puppy cuddling and dog patting later, with Dexter back in the kitchen and Gretel and her puppies safely tucked away in their pen, Nash drove us in his pickup truck to Mission Bay, a stunning white-sand beach in a well-heeled neighborhood, near the city's aquarium.

We parked and took a short stroll in the warm summer's evening to the large grassy area under the pohutukawas, New Zealand's Christmas trees, settling on a spot near the art deco fountain. It was late enough that there were only a few children still playing in its water, and despite the bustle across the street at the cafés, bars, and restaurants, it was a wonderfully tranquil and romantic spot.

Nash pulled a blue and green checkered blanket out of the old-fashioned cane picnic basket he had brought, and I helped him lay it out, placing the oversized cushions at the back edge so we could sit and look out at the beach and the island of Rangitoto beyond.

My tummy grumbled as I looked at the cheese, the French stick of bread, the hummus, the sliced ham, and the chocolate-dipped strawberries in front of me.

"That looks amazing."

"Dig in. Want another glass of wine? Well, it's a 'plastic' of wine, but that doesn't quite sound right, does it?"

"Sure, a 'plastic' of wine would be great."

We sat together and ate, drank, and chatted, enjoying the increasingly orange glow of the evening sun. Being as far south as New Zealand is, the summer sun doesn't set in Auckland until as late as quarter to nine, plenty of time to enjoy a leisurely picnic with a handsome and thoroughly swoon-worthy man, overlooking the water.

"Tell me, what do you do for a living?" I asked, picking one of the chocolate-dipped strawberries up in my hand. "I mean, I know you're a builder, working on that site on Jervois Road, but what exactly do you do?"

"I'm the site manager. I oversee all the work, make sure no one's being unsafe, that sort of thing."

"So, you get to boss people around?"

He chuckled. "Some of the time, yeah. My dad's the one who gets to do that all the time, though. He runs the business."

"Oh?" I had noticed the "Campbell Construction" sign on his truck and had assumed it was Nash's business.

"He's the Campbell in 'Campbell Construction.' You know you're sitting on the Campbell tartan?"

"I did not know that." I ran my hand over the woolen blanket. "It's nice. I like the blue."

"Dad's pretty keen on the whole Scottish roots thing. My mom is part Italian, so between the two of them, I get beaten about the head with traditions."

"That's great! Italian food and Scottish tartan." I chuckled. "We don't have any traditions in our family. Well, other than the usual Kiwi stuff of barbecues, jandals, and refusing to believe it ever gets cold here."

Right on cue, a cool breeze skimmed off the water and I shivered.

Nash reached over and rubbed my arm. "If I had a jacket, I'd give it to you."

"No problem." I shivered again. Now that the sun had almost set and the nearby fountain had begun its evening light show, my sleeveless shirt felt woefully inadequate.

"How about we pack this basket up and go for a drink at one of the places across the road?"

"That sounds wonderful."

We packed the picnic basket and returned it to the car, walking along the road hand in hand. We found a bar, a little quieter than many, and ordered a couple of drinks. With no place free to sit, we stood together, so close we were almost touching. It felt like we were in a little bubble, the rest of the world carrying on, doing its own thing, as we reveled in one another's company.

"I've been thinking about you and this singing thing," Nash said.

"You have?"

"Remember how you told me you didn't have the courage to do it?"

"Yes," I replied cautiously.

"Well, I think you should go for it."

I ran my finger around the top of my glass. "You do, huh?"

"Yes. I do. I think you should stand up and sing for an audience. Although, maybe I should hear you sing in the shower first, just to be sure."

I slapped him playfully on the arm. "One day . . . maybe."

He raised his eyebrows at me suggestively and my belly did a flip-flop. There was no denying I was very attracted to Nash. In fact, I would challenge most women not to be: he was tall, athletic, charming, and sweet. Plus, *he looked like Jon Snow*! But the last thing I wanted to do was to rush things with him.

As I looked into his eyes, something in my chest moved. "I'll think about it."

"Oh, come on! Sing something for me."

I looked around at the busy bar. "Here?"

"Why not?"

I laughed. "You won't be able to hear me for a start. Which, come to think of it, may not be a bad thing."

"I bet you've got a beautiful voice."

"You're a total charmer, you know that?"

He shrugged. "I may be."

The music changed to an upbeat song I recognized from the radio.

"I love this song!" Nash declared.

"Me, too."

"Come, dance with me." He took me by the hand and nodded over at the dance floor where a group of maybe a dozen people were dancing.

"Sure!" I placed my glass on the counter, and we made our way through the throngs to the dance floor. When we got there, Nash began to move his body to the music, and I watched him, my lips pressed together. Nash was a super-hot guy, good-looking, masculine, all the things I liked in a man. But could he dance? No, siree.

Nash dances like Carlton from The Fresh Prince of Bel-Air.

I stifled a laugh. So as not to raise any questions, I began to dance too, although I found it hard to look at him with my giggles threatening to escape at any moment. I may not have been about to win *Dancing with the Stars*, but I didn't look like Nash.

We danced until the music changed to a song I didn't recognize. Fearing a potential return of the freak-out, I suggested we get a drink of water and talk some more. Luckily, Nash agreed, and I could feel the anxiety over his enthusiastic Carlton-esque dancing begin to dissipate.

"What's Nash short for?" I asked, once we had our glasses of water and found a quieter spot to talk.

"Guess," he replied, waggling his eyebrows.

"Err . . . Nashville?"

He shook his head.

"Nashton?" Another shake. I was running out of ideas. "Nashterton?" Okay, I was getting silly now.

"Is that even a name?"

"Err . . . how about Nasher?"

He let out a low, sexy laugh. It made the hairs on the back of my neck stand on end. "That one sounds like something to do with teeth. I'll put you out of your misery. It's none of the above. It's just Nash."

"Well, then, 'Just Nash,' I've had a wonderful evening. Thank you."

"Yeah, me too." He placed his hand on my arm, leaned in, and kissed me. "What are you doing next Saturday?"

"Seeing you?" I hazarded.

His grin gave me all the response I needed. "I have an idea. I'll text you with the details. Keep Saturday afternoon free."

"All right."

We walked to his car, and he drove me back to my apartment. Parked outside my building, I reached across and slipped my hand around his neck, pulling him in for a kiss. Once again, it was amazing, and once again, I swore I saw stars.

"Good night," I said through the open window once I was out of the car. Putting a hunk of metal between me and the hunk in the truck felt like a very good move on my part.

"I'll see you next weekend. That is, if you don't happen to pass a certain construction site on Jervois Road between now and then."

I beamed at him. "We'll have to see about that."

I turned and walked on legs that felt like jelly up the steps and into my apartment building. As I held the door open, I turned back and saw him sitting in his truck, watching me, that goofy grin on his handsome face once more.

I had made the right choice, and it looked like this Last First Date thing may work out perfectly, after all.

CHAPTER 8

*a*s I walked up the stairs of my apartment building, I could still feel Nash's lips on mine. It was the perfect end to the perfect evening with the perfect guy. How had I managed to find him, Bailey had asked? Right now, I had no idea, but I was deeply thankful I had. Not only was he everything I could hope for, he got me, meeting my commitment-phobia head on. Maybe Paige was right? Maybe there was one perfect guy out there for all of us, just waiting to be found.

And a small voice inside of me told me I'd found mine.

As I rounded the corner, I could hear a TV blaring from one of the apartments above. I walked up the final flight and realized with a shock the noise was coming from my own apartment, and not only that, there were loud voices added to the TV din.

I unlocked my front door and pushed the door open to be met with the sight of my brother and three other guys sprawled over my beautiful furniture, drinking and talking loudly over the top of a rugby match being played on the big screen TV.

I let the door slam behind me, but no one even noticed. They were too engrossed in their drunken banter—which completely lacked in wit, despite the fact they laughed at what each other said. I dropped my purse on the kitchen counter and walked over to them. Still unnoticed, I picked up the remote and switched the TV off. *That got their attention.* They all turned with a start to look at me.

"Oh, hey, sis! Everyone, this is my little sis," Ryan slurred from his spot on the sofa—the very spot he was in when I had gone out on my date five hours ago. I wondered how he had managed to get all the takeout and collect three drunken friends without moving.

"What's going on, Ryan?" I asked, my hands on my hips like I was Mom, scolding her naughty son. Which is exactly how I felt, only Ryan was my big brother and had always been Mr. Golden Child in that highly responsible and successful way firstborn offspring often are.

"Hanging with these guys," he replied, gesturing to the motley collection of men currently messing up my once pristine living room. "Hey, do you want a drink? We've got beers, right, guys?"

"Yeah!" one of them replied with gusto. He was half sitting and half lying across one of my armchairs, his feet dangling down the side. His T-shirt didn't quite cover his midriff, and I caught sight of his pale, hairy belly poking out the bottom.

I shot him a dirty look and returned my attention to my brother. "Ryan? A word?" I asked, my voice like steel.

"Sure. What is it?" he asked, taking another swig of his beer. Half of the drink missed his mouth and instead ran down his chin and onto his T-shirt, leaving a growing wet patch across his chest. It was as disgusting as it sounded.

I looked around the room at the men. They all appeared to be as inebriated as Ryan; a large collection of empty bottles scattered across the floor. One of them looked like he might have nodded off to sleep, lounging on the sofa next to Ryan. There was even a pair of dirty socks slung across one of my lampshades. What had they been doing for socks to land there? I decided I didn't want to know. I pursed my lips. "I'd like to speak to you alone, please."

"Anything you have to say can be said in front of my crew, right, guys?" Ryan replied.

"Yeah!" Hairy Gut Guy repeated—until he looked up at me. "I mean, that's fine with me." He shot me a weak smile. I didn't return it.

"All right, then. I want you all to leave. Now."

"But, sis," Ryan whined.

"No buts! Just do it!"

I really do sound like Mom.

"All right, guys, I guess we should call it a night," Hairy Gut Guy said, shooting me an apologetic look. Maybe he thought by helping me out I wouldn't kill him? I was still undecided.

"Thank you," I said, mustering as much control as I could manage.

Finally, once the men had gone and it was just Ryan and me, filling the recycling bins with empty bottles and pizza boxes, I asked him what he had been thinking, bringing those gross men into my home.

"I thought you'd be happy."

"On what planet would I be happy that you and your he-men friends messed up my living room? I mean," I added, pointing to a splotch of something unidentifiable on one of my armchairs, "look at this! It's ruined."

"I meant because I wasn't just sitting around, feeling sorry for myself."

I stood up straight and looked at him. "Oh." I felt bad. Ryan had been in such a funk over his relationship breakup, it hadn't occurred to me that this evening was some sort of progress for him. "Sorry."

He slumped down onto one of the armchairs, landed on an empty bottle, pulled it out from underneath himself, and dropped it into the bin. He let out a sigh. "I know what you're going to say."

"You do?" I asked, crouching down next to him and trying not to breathe in his scent, a combination of pepperoni pizza, garlic bread, and stale beer. *Ugh.*

"'Getting wasted isn't the answer,'" he said with air quotes. "But you know what, sis? Sometimes it *is* the answer."

I noticed tears welling in his eyes and it got me, right in the heart. Ryan was my older brother, I don't remember the last time I saw him cry. He had always been strong and stoical, his life under control, with him in the driver's seat. Not . . . this.

Despite his stench, I hugged him in close. "Maybe you're right," I said softly, wishing I could take his hurt away for him.

I found a box of tissues, obscured by a banana peel (really?), and handed him a wad. He took them and wiped his eyes in the way guys do, like they're angry with their face. Women dab, men scrape. On this score, I was more than happy to be a woman.

"Did something happen?" I asked once he was more composed. Ryan had been more than a little maudlin since he arrived, but he hadn't been hitting the bottle—or bottles, as was the case tonight.

He studied his hands for a long time, then glanced up at me, and back down again. "Amelia's seeing someone else."

"What?" I screeched. Clearing my throat, I said in a calmer voice, "I mean, so soon? She's not hanging around." Ryan and Amelia had only broken up a matter of about a month ago. For her to have moved on this quickly seemed more than a little suspicious to me. Maybe she'd developed feelings for someone else while she was still with Ryan? Or, worse yet, maybe she'd even had an *affair*.

"Yeah," he replied glumly.

"Are you sure? I mean, how do you know?"

"Greg saw her with some guy last night at a bar."

"He might have been a work colleague?" I suggested.

"They were kissing."

"Ah." Not a work colleague, then. Or at least, not the type of work colleague I had.

I rubbed his forearm. "I'm sorry, Ryan. That really sucks."

"Yeah, it does." He let out a heavy sigh. "Anyway, enough about me and my crap life. How was your date?"

I thought of Nash, and I couldn't help a smile spreading across my face. "It was nice."

"This was with the dog guy, right?"

"Nash, yes. But he's more than just 'the dog guy.' He's smart and kind and fun. He did this picnic for us, and it was so romantic." I let out a contented sigh.

"Sounds like someone's smitten."

I shrugged, a few butterflies batting their wings inside at the thought. "Maybe." I shrugged, trying to appear nonchalant. "And I know what you're going to say: 'it'll end in heartbreak.' But I've decided to give it a shot anyway."

And I had. For better or for worse, as the saying goes.

"Good for you."

"What? No 'love is for wimps,' no 'it's doomed from the start,' no 'it's all a waste of time'?" I replied, quoting a few of Ryan's favorite current sayings.

Really, he'd been a wonderful roommate to have around.

Ryan managed a short-lived smile as he knitted his eyebrows together. "It's love, is it?"

I could feel a blush form on my cheeks as my heart beat in my ears. *Love?* Was he certifiably *insane?* "Oh, it's far too early to say. This was only our third date."

"Well, that's two more dates with the same guy than you usually manage," he replied, pushing himself up off the sofa to a standing position. "Woah," he muttered, grabbing onto the arm of the chair. "Make the room stop spinning, would you?"

I took him by the arm and led him to the bathroom. "Go, wash up. I'll get the sofa bed ready for you. And a large glass of water."

He leaned up against the bathroom door frame. "You know it's doomed."

"Yeah, sure." I smiled at him.

I waited until he was in the bathroom and had closed the door before I set about getting my living room back to the way it should look and making up Ryan's bed for him. My big brother may be bitter and twisted, but I had a new-found seed of hope inside of me.

I was beginning to believe in love again, and this time, I wanted my happily ever after.

* * *

MONDAY MORNING ROLLED AROUND and I was sitting at our usual table by the window at the Cozy Cottage Café with Cassie, when Bailey arrived to deliver our morning treats.

"A slice of flourless raspberry and chocolate cake for you," Bailey said, placing the cake in front of Cassie, "and a slice of orange and almond syrup cake for you."

"Thanks," we both said, smiling up at her.

"I'll be right back with your coffees," Bailey added.

"Then, you can help me quiz Marissa on her *third* date with Nash," Cassie said with a smirk.

After I'd informed the girls of my second date success with Nash at Alessandro's, they made me promise to give them a full debrief after Saturday night's big date. Although I intended to keep some of the more personal details to myself, I was as eager as a child at Christmas to tell them how it went.

Bailey raised her eyebrows, her eyes wide. "Third? Oh, this I want to hear. Don't you dare start until I'm back."

I shook my head, grinning, warmth spreading through my belly. "I won't, I promise."

I turned to Cassie. "I guess we'll have to talk work, then."

"Actually, I'm interested to know what you think of Antoinette? You know, I can't say her name without imagining her with her head chopped off."

I let out a giggle. "Poor girl. You can't blame her for her name."

"True. So, how is she?"

"You know, I think she's all right. She's eager to learn and really quite sweet. With the right training, she might just shape up to be an asset to the team"

"That's great to hear. I've had my doubts. Are you happy to have her tag along on a few more of your meetings this week?"

Thanks to Nash—who I had been texting up a flirtatious storm with since our last date—I was in a generous mood. "Sure, why not?"

"Did I miss anything?" Bailey said as she placed our cups of coffee in front of us.

"Nothing," Cassie replied.

"Good, because I only have a few moments and Paige made me promise to report everything back in full."

I looked over at the counter, where Paige and Sophie were busy serving customers. I caught Paige's eye and gave her the thumbs-up.

She beamed back at me, clearly getting the message my date went well, before returning her attention to the task at hand.

"So?" Bailey led.

My face broke into a smile the size of Texas. "It was perfect."

"Perfect?" Cassie asked, her eyes huge as Bailey put her hand on her heart and sighed.

I nodded. "Yes. He picked me up, and we went to his house first where I got to meet the most adorable puppies I've ever seen."

"Puppies? I love puppies," Bailey gushed.

I chuckled. "Who doesn't?"

"What type were they?"

"Nash said they weren't one hundred percent sure, but the mother is an abandoned German Shepherd."

"Were they all squishy and wriggly and lick-y and cute?" Bailey asked.

"Oh, my, yes! Super, super cute. You'll have to come see them, Bailey, you would die."

"Hey, you two," Cassie said, her hands in the "stop" sign. "Can we focus on the actual date here? I have a meeting shortly, and Marissa has a lot of work to do."

"Sorry. Okay, as I said, the date started when I met the puppies and it was all good."

"You're completely over Slobbergate, then?" Bailey asked.

"I am," I replied with a smile. "Then, get this, he'd packed a picnic basket with a blanket and pillows and yummy food, and we went to Mission Bay where we sat together, watching the sun set, talking. It was wonderful," I said with a smile. "Well, other than Nash's dancing. He dances like Carlton."

"Carlton?" Cassie questioned.

"You know, from *The Fresh Prince of Bel-Air*?"

"Oh. That's not good," Cassie replied, shaking her head.

"No, but you know what? In the past, that kind of thing would have had me running for the hills. Literally. But now?" I shrugged. "It doesn't matter. I still want to date him."

Cassie sat back in her seat, sizing me up. "Marissa Jones: all grown up."

I let out a light laugh. She was right, I had grown up. I wanted to be with Nash—I was going to do my best to make it work.

"You see? Right there. That look on your face. That's what I want," Bailey said.

"She's fallen for him, that's for sure," Cassie said, grinning at me.

"Oh, I don't know about that yet. It's early days," I protested, even though I knew it myself. I slid my fork into my cake and took a bite, hoping to deflect attention from me. "Bailey, this is extra good today."

"It's because you're in *lurve*," Cassie teased. "Everything seems better."

I shot her a look. I turned to Bailey and asked, "Have you ever tried speed dating?"

"Speed dating?" Bailey guffawed. "No!"

"Isn't that a bit nineties?" Cassie asked.

"I guess. I saw an advertisement for a speed dating night at O'Dowd's." I thought back to my date at the bar with Blaze. Wow, that felt so long ago. "I thought of you, now that you're looking for your Last First Date, too."

"I'm not sure it's really my style," Bailey replied, looking dubious.

"Actually, I think it's perfect," Cassie said, leaning forward in her chair. "Think about it, Bailey. That way, you can date any number of guys, all in one evening."

"Maybe," she replied noncommittally. "Anyway, now that I have all the date gossip, I think I'd better get back to it. I'm sure Paige and Sophie need my help." She stood up and slipped her chair under our table. "I'm really happy for you, Marissa. You deserve this."

I beamed at her. What had started out as a knee-jerk reaction to Eddie's engagement announcement had turned into something so much more.

And I couldn't wait to see where it went.

CHAPTER 9

*T*he rest of my week was spent either with customers or working on projects for my customers, with Antoinette shadowing my every move. She was a fast learner and kept quiet during meetings, allowing me to get on with my job. If I had to have someone with me, I couldn't have hoped for anyone better.

"I loved the way you handled that complaint back there," Antoinette said as we were walking through the city on our way back from a meeting. "You were 'firm but fair,' as my aunt would say."

I smiled at her, knowing full well she was referring to Laura Carmichael, my boss's boss—so far up the AGD food chain from me, it gave me a nosebleed. "Well, your aunt knows what she's talking about."

"Oh, she sure does. She's amazing. She's my role model, well, one of them, that is." She looked at me through her lashes.

"It's great to have role models. Something to aspire to," I replied.

"Don't you want to know who the other one is?"

"Sure." I knew she was going to tell me regardless.

"You, silly!" she said with a slap to my arm.

"Oh! That's so sweet of you, thank you," I said with genuine surprise. Although I had spent a lot of time training Antoinette, it didn't occur to me for a moment she would see me as a role model. I was just doing the job Cassie had asked me to do.

"Of course. I want to be just like you. You're so in control and poised and nothing seems to rattle you."

"Well, I wouldn't say *nothing* rattles—"

"And everyone on the team respects you," she continued, cutting me off, "especially Cassie. And the guys listen to what you have to say in meetings. You're *such* a role model, I'm surprised you didn't know that."

"I've enjoyed having you work with me this week, Antoinette." The unadulterated praise was making me a little uncomfortable. "Hey, do you feel like grabbing a take-out coffee?" As it happened, we were only a block or so away from the Cozy Cottage and I could do with a caffeine fix. "I know a great place just a block that way." I pointed up the street.

"Sure! I'd love that. Yes!" She punched the air in a cutesy way, much like many of the female tennis pros did when they won a game.

I shot her a sideways look. I'd give her one thing, she was enthusiastic.

We took the short stroll, Antoinette continuing to stroke my ego, telling me how much she admired the way I'd handled certain issues with one customer, the way in which I had pitched a solution upgrade to another customer. It felt nice but a little too much, like I was the best thing since ice cream.

We arrived at the Cozy Cottage and walked past the café patrons, enjoying their coffee in the warm afternoon sun, and through the open front door. I spotted Bailey at the counter, handing some change over to a customer. When she saw me, her face lit up into her habitual smile.

"Marissa! What a lovely surprise."

I greeted Bailey and introduced her to Antoinette. In her figure-hugging clothing with heavy makeup and her long platinum blond hair extensions, she looked a little cheap next to Bailey's classic Italian beauty.

Bailey was her usual affable self, welcoming Antoinette to the café.

"I've never been here," Antoinette said, looking around the café. "It's so ... cozy!"

Bailey and I both laughed. "It's named correctly, then," Bailey replied.

"Oh, this place is called 'Cozy'?" Antoinette asked.

"It's the Cozy Cottage Café. It's the best café in Auckland," I replied.

We placed our take-out orders and Antoinette insisted on paying. "It's the least I can do for you, *role model*," she said, her eyes shining. Her phone rang, diverting her attention. "Oh, do you mind? I have to take this."

I nodded at her. "Sure." To be fair, I was happy for the break in her veneration. I was beginning to feel like I was some sort of important spiritual leader or something, not just an account manager doing her job.

"She's perky," Bailey said with a wry grin.

I rolled my eyes. "It's like having a team of cheer-leaders trail behind me, cheering my every move." I glanced at Antoinette, leaning up against the end of the counter.

"And she's popular," Bailey added, nodding at a table of two businessmen who were unabashedly watching Antoinette's every move.

I let out a sigh. "I tried to talk to her about dressing more appropriately."

Bailey smiled at me. "We all have our own style, and she seems nice."

That was my friend, Bailey, always so positive and open-minded. She and Paige were cut from the same sweet and kind piece of cloth. No wonder they were perfect business partners, running the Cozy Cottage.

"I almost forgot. A guy came in looking for you earlier. Said his name was Brian, I think?" Bailey said.

"Brian? I don't know a Brian."

"I may have got the name wrong. Ryan?"

"Was he stooped over, a bit gray, and otherwise downtrodden looking?"

"Actually, he was, now that you mention it."

"That's my brother."

"Oh." Bailey pulled a face.

"Bad breakup."

"Ah."

"He's taking it hard."

"I get that. Poor guy. He seemed nice."

I looked at her sideways and thought I detected a hint of a flush on her pretty face. "Euw! He's my brother!"

The color in Bailey's cheeks deepened a touch. "I didn't mean anything by that. He was sweet, that's all."

"And broken. Totally broken." I shook my head for emphasis.

She scrunched up her face. "Poor guy."

"He's not a *guy*. He's my brother."

She laughed. "You know what I mean. Anyway, were you meant to meet him here? Only, I didn't think you all allowed men at the Cozy Cottage?"

"Well, as a rule, we don't. And no, I wasn't."

When we first started coming to the Cozy Cottage Café, Cassie, Paige, and I had decided immediately it was going to be our special place, no men allowed. It was kind of like a sanctuary for us, away from work, families, dating, and all that drama. We had agreed it was too special to share, and we would only ever bring a guy here when we were certain he was The One.

"But, as I said before, Ryan is my brother. He doesn't count. Plus, he came to find me, technically I didn't bring him here." I wondered why Ryan hadn't just called me. I pulled my phone out of my purse and checked my messages. Nothing from him. I'd call him later.

"Here you go," Sophie said with a smile, handing me two cups of take-out coffee. "Sugar and sweetener is here," she added, gesturing to some bowls on the counter. "Help yourself."

"Thanks, Sophie," I replied. Sophie was one of those sweet, friendly baristas you often don't encounter downtown. Here they were usually major hipsters, with their retro clothing, elaborate facial hair—for the men, obviously—and cooler than cool attitudes. Sophie was the perfect addition to the Paige-Bailey partnership: low on pretention and high on great food, good service, and a warm and welcoming attitude.

Antoinette appeared at my side. "Oh, I totally forgot to pay. I'm sorry. Next one's on me."

"Sure."

"I've been thinking," Antoinette began, stirring three packets of sugar (three!) into her coffee, "how would you feel about me helping you do the big pitch to Pukeko Chocolates next week? I think it would be super useful for me and great experience."

"Oh." There was too much at stake to allow a new recruit any input on this one. I turned and waved goodbye to Bailey as Antoinette replaced the cap on her coffee cup. We turned to leave. I chose my words carefully. "Look, Antoinette, I think you're doing so well, and I'm really impressed with your work ethic and commitment to your new job."

"I can feel a 'but' coming," she said as we walked past the outdoor tables.

"You're right, there is a 'but.' I would like to handle this one myself." I thought about something that would appease her, a smaller account where there was less at stake. "How about you come to my meeting with another customer this afternoon? They are looking for a new data solution, and I think you could add some value there."

She shrugged, clearly disappointed. "Sure, that would be great. Look, I don't want to step on your toes or anything. I just want to get as much experience as I can before I get my own customer portfolio."

I smiled at her. "I get that. Let's get back to the office and plan out how we'll run this meeting this afternoon, okay?"

"Sure. One thing. Is it okay if I head home for an early lunch? I'll be back at my desk within the hour, I promise."

"You don't need to ask *me*, I'm not your boss."

"You kind of are, or at least, that's how I see you."

Wow, this girl was good.

"It's not a problem with me. I'll see you back in the office."

I walked the rest of the way, enjoying my solitude—well, as much solitude as you can get in downtown Auckland on a weekday—and ran through the presentation I was planning to give to Pukeko Chocolates in my mind. I made a few mental notes as I went. Of course, my mind kept darting back to Nash, but I reined it back in, reminding myself I had a job to do and a huge deal to land.

By the time I was back in the office, a good twenty minutes' walk from the Cozy Cottage, I was almost positive Pukeko would be signing on the dotted line before the month was out. I just needed to get them over that line. I thought of their logo with the long-limbed native bird. I wanted this deal more than anything.

I went straight to my desk and downloaded all the ideas I'd had on my walk, adjusting my presentation, and firing technical questions off to Bryce to ensure my ideas would work.

When I finally came up for air, I got up to stretch my legs and grab a glass of water from the water cooler. I noticed a woman I'd never seen before, sitting at Antoinette's desk, peering at her computer.

"Ah, excuse me?" I said, approaching Antoinette's desk. "I'm not sure you should be looking at that."

The woman swiveled around in the chair and smiled at me. "Hi, Marissa."

My jaw dropped open. It was Antoinette, only this person didn't look anything like her. She was wearing an outfit that wouldn't have looked out of place in the Amish community—if they had platinum blond women with hair extensions there, that was. She was wearing a cover-all, olive sack-like dress, flat shoes, minimal makeup, and her hair was tied up in a severe bun. All that was missing from the ensemble was a bonnet, a pitchfork, and a horse and carriage.

"Antoinette. You look . . . different," I managed.

She smoothed her already incredibly neat hair, patting her platinum bun. "I'm taking your advice. You said, 'dress as unsexy as you can,' and I figured this"—she glanced down at her baggy dress—"was pretty unsexy."

I was still slack-jawed, trying to get my head around the transformation. "I'm not sure I used those exact words."

"Oh, you definitely did." She nodded at me, raising her eyebrows.

"Well, I know I didn't say dress like a nineteenth-century mission-ary!" Not that I had anything against nineteenth-century missionaries, of course. I'm sure they did some wonderful work, only, you didn't come across them in corporate New Zealand all that often these days.

"Oh, Marissa, you are silly." She shook her head. "I'm just trying to emulate you, my role model."

I looked down at my own outfit. Although I wasn't anywhere near the "put it all on display" ballpark Antoinette usually hung around in, I was equally far from looking like she did right now. I was a pencil skirt, heels, and blouse kind of girl at work, a cute jacket in winter. "Okay," I replied, uncertainly. "Thanks . . . I guess."

I almost regretted talking to her about her appearance, although to be fair, she *had* asked me about it.

Hadn't she?

She flashed her smile. Without that shovel-full of makeup, she actually looked really pretty.

"So, we're going to the client soon?" I nodded in response. She pulled out a notepad and pen. "Tell me all about it."

We went to the empty conference room, people shooting us quizzical looks as we walked across the sales team floor together. I took her through what we were trying to do with the customer this afternoon, suggesting she talk about our customer service offering while I tacked the solution details.

"I would be honored," she replied.

"Great." I formed my face into what I hoped was a smile as I wondered about Antoinette's sanity. She was clearly a woman of extremes, throwing herself with happy abandon at an idea. We'd gone from Pamela Anderson to Mother Theresa with enough speed to give a girl whiplash, and I was still trying to wrap my head around it.

Later that afternoon, and with a nervous knot in my belly, Amish Antoinette and I went to see Storage Plus, the customer we had been preparing for. I would love to have said her appearance didn't turn heads and raise a few eyebrows, but that would be a barefaced lie. Storage Plus hadn't seen Pam Anderson Antoinette, so I wondered if they simply assumed she was from some unusual religious sect. Whatever they thought, they simply went with it and seemed more than happy with our presentation. Antoinette nailed her section—which I heaved a huge sigh of relief over, I can tell you—and we left with a verbal agreement to proceed, subject to contract conditions.

All in all, despite Antoinette's strange transformation, the afternoon had worked out very nicely indeed. Things felt like they were on the up-and-up for me: Nash, work, everything.

It was almost too good to be true.

CHAPTER 10

Saturday finally came around and it was time for date number four with Nash. I had impressed myself—and everyone else—by not having even one freak-out moment during the week. In fact, I had been quite the opposite. Every time I had thought of Nash, my chest would expand and my tummy would do flips.

"Are you going to tell me where we're going?" I asked, sitting in the passenger seat of Nash's pickup truck as we made our way through Auckland's busy Saturday traffic. "I think I spied your picnic basket in the back. Please tell me we're going on another picnic and you didn't just leave that in there with the old food and dirty dishes from last weekend, because that would be super gross."

Nash chuckled. The rich, deep sound made me warm inside. His laugh was something I absolutely loved about him. The way his eyes crinkled and his low, husky laugh reverberated through me . . .

Back up the bus. Had I just said "love"?

"It's full of fresh food and wine and Diet Coke and *cleaned* dishes, so you can relax," he replied.

I cleared my throat. "That's good to hear." Yes, I would think about food, not my feelings. Much safer. "So, where are we headed?"

Nash expertly backed the truck into a parallel park and switched the ignition off. "Here."

I peered out the windows at the busy shopping street, full of boutiques and cafés and fashionably dressed people. "Parnell?" I asked, totally confused. "It's not exactly known as the city's top spot for relaxed picnic dates, you know."

He laughed again, and my heart melted once more. *Wow, have I fallen for this guy already?*

"Trust me," he said with a wink.

"Okay," I replied uncertainly. I opened my door and hopped out onto the sidewalk. After the puppies wrecked my white skirt on our last date, I knew better than to wear typical date clothes with Nash. This time, I was dressed in a pair of skinny jeans, flats, a cute, loose top, and a long necklace.

With the picnic basket in one hand, Nash took mine in his other and we sauntered along the street together.

"Do we get to see the pups later?"

"Absolutely. They've been asking after you."

"They have?" An image of the puppies requesting my presence popped into my head. They may have been wearing top hats and monocles in this image, and yes, my imagination had totally run away with me. "No, you're being silly."

"Marissa, of course I'm being silly. They're puppies, they can't talk." He paused, bent down, and kissed me on the lips.

As he pulled away, I let out a contented sigh. *So, this is what it feels like to be happy.* Not that we'd had that "let's date exclusively" conversation or anything. But I for one couldn't imagine wanting to date anyone else. This simply felt too good, too right.

Maybe I had fallen for him?

In fact, I realized with a start, I hadn't even checked Eddie's Facebook page since Nash's and my last date. *Huh.* Not checking up to see what Eddie was doing? That was major progress for me. I had to admit, I was proud of myself.

We walked hand-in-hand down the street, past the boutiques,

cafés, and restaurants, turning off and heading toward The Domain, a large, leafy, green park near Parnell.

"Oh, I know where we're going! A picnic in the park."

"With music," he added. "We're going to see Joey Cruikshank and Vi Edwards in concert at the Rotunda."

"We are?" My eyes got huge. Joey Cruikshank and Vi Edwards were two popular New Zealand musicians who sang beautiful ballads. Their music was so chill, perfect for a Saturday afternoon date with Nash. "Oh, that's amazing. Thank you!"

"I thought you might like them."

We arrived at the Rotunda where there was a sea of people, picnic blankets, and low chairs. The atmosphere was relaxed and happy—reflecting my own. We found a spot on the grass and set up. This time Nash had brought roast turkey and salad sandwiches with focaccia bread, some bagel chips and dip, and more of those delicious chocolate-dipped strawberries.

I surveyed the spread. "You're quite handy in the kitchen, aren't you?"

"I'd love to claim this was all me, but I bought it from the deli near my house."

"So, you're not quite the perfect guy?"

"Close?" He shrugged.

We sat back and began to eat, chatting about our weeks and people watching, one of my favorite pastimes at these events. I was still marveling at how easy this was with him, how it hadn't even occurred to me to let anything about him bother me, like it had on our first date.

After we'd cleaned up the sandwiches, we fed one another the strawberries, laughing at how cheesy it was—cheesy and incredibly sexy, I would add. Despite being out in public, surrounded by a few thousand people, we lay facing one another, propped up on our elbows, side-by-side, our bare toes touching.

"You know what?" He smiled at me.

"What?"

"I like you, Marissa Jones."

The trio of tap-dancing hamsters resumed their routine in my belly. "I like you, too, Nash Campbell."

He reached across and touched his fingers to my face. As he looked at me, his eyes were intense with the electricity that was zapping between us. I pushed myself up on my elbow and leaned down to kiss him. We were so lost in one another, we didn't even notice the musicians arrived on the stage until the crowd around us erupted into claps and cheers.

"I guess we should sit up and listen," I said.

"Shame. Kissing you has to be one of my favorite things to do."

We clapped along with the crowd as Vi Edwards stood on the stage in front of the microphone, her guitar slung across her body, looking every bit the folk music artist she was. As she began to play the first few chords of her latest release, the crowd erupted into fresh cheers. I couldn't help but sing along.

"You know you're good at this, right?" Nash said loudly in my ear during the chorus of "My Sweet Angel."

"At what? Singing along to Vi Edwards's music? Yeah, I think you're right!"

"I mean just *singing*. You have a beautiful voice."

"Aw, you're just saying that because I'm such a good kisser," I joked as heat rose in my cheeks.

I knew I had a nice enough voice, and I could carry a tune. I had been one of those nerdy teenagers who loved being in choirs. I was a second soprano and used to travel the country competing in choral competitions, and sometimes we would even win. I had loved it, and it gave me a sense of belonging, a much-needed purpose during the craziness of puberty.

The song ended, and people around us clapped and cheered.

"No, really. I think you should do this Friday night gig thing at your friend's place."

"Cozy Cottage Jam," I corrected him, my belly twisting into a knot, right on cue.

"Whatever," he said with a chortle, shaking his head. "I think you should do it. 'Feel the fear and do it anyway,' and other inspirational bumper stickers."

Feel the fear was right.

"Paige and Bailey have probably got their sessions fully booked by now, and I'm not a professional singer! I mean, yeah, I like it, but that's hardly enough to . . . to get up in front of a roomful of people and sing."

He turned to face me as the musicians started up the next song. "Have you finished?"

"Then there's the fact I don't have any material. I don't even think I know all the words to any songs."

"Anything else?"

I looked back at Nash. He raised his eyebrows at me, locking his eyes onto mine. I tried to think of something, but in the end, I simply shook my head as the knot wound around again inside.

He put his hands on my arms, fixing me with his stare. "You know those are all just excuses. You're passionate about singing, you told me so. Why don't you just forget all this crap and give it a shot?"

I opened my mouth to respond. I knew I was out of reasons. As I looked at his smiling face, a little seed of excitement began to grow inside me. Could I do it? Could I stand up in front of an audience and sing? It was something I had always imagined myself doing when I was a teenager. I would fantasize I had miraculously lost forty pounds overnight and had become a Faith Hill look-alike, captivating an audience with my voice and beauty.

"I . . . I," I stammered.

"Say yes," Nash encouraged.

"Yes," I said in a little voice, my lips forming a small smile.

He cupped his ear with his hand. "I'm sorry, what did you say?"

"Yes!" I yelled, laughing.

We high-fived. "You are not going to regret this."

It may have been Nash, the music, the ambience, I don't know. But in that moment, I believed him. I could do it, I could sing at the Cozy Cottage Jam, even if it scared the living daylights out of me.

We spent most of Joey Cruikshank's set swaying to his music and cleaning up the last of the strawberries. A few songs in, it began to cloud over, and there was a sudden distinct chill in the air.

"I think it's going to rain," Nash said, looking up at the looming dark clouds.

That's the thing in Auckland: you can start the day off in brilliant and gorgeously warm weather, by lunch, it's raining, and then it's hot and humid for the afternoon. The song "Four Seasons in One Day" was written about this place, for good reason.

A few drops landed on our bare arms, and then the heavens opened their floodgates.

My hair!

I spent time every morning straightening out my bobbed locks, ensuring they fell just so. Rain was the enemy. It made my hair look like it could comfortably house a large family of birds inside. Not pretty, not pretty at all. Not a lot of people had seen the natural state of my hair, and I wasn't about to let Nash see it today.

We quickly grabbed the food wrappers and drink bottles and stashed them safely away in the picnic basket. Nash scooped the blanket off the ground, and we sat side-by-side on the grass, huddled under it, listening to the music as people near us scattered far and wide.

It was so romantic, just the two of us—that and a bit smelly and damp. The rain refused to let up, and after a while, it began to seep through the blanket where our bodies touched it. Growing increasingly uncomfortable, I reached up and smoothed down my hair. It was only a matter of time before it brought new depth of meaning to the word "frizz." I needed the rain to let up so I could get back to the truck safely.

In the end, I had no choice. We beat a hasty retreat, back to the sanctuary of Nash's truck, me holding the picnic blanket over my head. Once inside, smelling of the rain, I pulled down the visor and peered in the mirror. My hair could give Little Orphan Annie a run for her money right now. I scrunched up my eyes and snapped the visor shut. *Dammit!*

"Well, that was wet. Do you think it's puppy time?" Nash said, turning and smiling at me. I noticed his expression changed as he took in my bedraggled appearance.

Despite willing him not to notice my hair, I knew he had. How could he miss me looking like I'd joined an eighties soft rock band? "Don't say anything!" I warned.

A smile teased the edges of his mouth. "Nothing?"

I pursed my lips and shook my head, angry. "I hate my hair."

His brows knitted together, he reached his hand across and took a curl in his fingers. "Why?"

"Why? Are you *serious?*" I asked, almost choking. He had to be teasing me, and I didn't like it one little bit.

"Yes, I am serious. Okay, it's bigger than you usually wear it, but it looks great. Wild, I guess."

I harrumphed.

He slid his hand around the back of my head and brushed his lips against mine. "And really, really sexy."

"It does?" I squeaked.

"It does."

And just to prove it, he kissed me again, tangling his fingers in my hair, making my whole body tingle.

Eventually, after I'd seen every star in the galaxy dance before my eyes, he said, "You should wear it like this."

I shook my head. Nash may like my hair in its natural state, but I wasn't anywhere near "there" yet. "Maybe," I replied noncommittally.

"Do you still want to go see the puppies?"

My face broke into a grin. "Oh, yes."

Nash drove slowly through the wet streets, his hand in mine. I watched him, his free hand on the steering wheel, wondering how I had found such a man, a man who accepted my flaws, who was patient with me, who even liked my crazy-ass hair.

I had to be the luckiest girl in the world.

We arrived at Nash's place and dashed through the rain from the driveway to his front door. He got us some towels to dry off, and I could hear the puppies crying at the living room door. I couldn't help but grin. Although I'd only met them once, they had made a significant impression on me. They were so happy, so eager, so inquisitive. They made me warm inside in a way very few things did.

Other than Nash.

"Are you ready for this?" he asked, his hand on the doorknob.

I grinned. "Definitely."

A moment later, the door swung wide, I was on the hardwood floor being mobbed by five enthusiastic puppies. They licked and squirmed and whined and did everything they'd done the time I'd met them, right down to the slobber on my pants.

"Feel like a cup of coffee?" Nash offered once we and the puppies were in his living room, the door closed safely behind us.

"Sure, that would be great."

With Nash in the kitchen, I returned my attention to the pups. I spotted the one I'd cuddled the last time and collected her up. I grinned at her, tickling her tummy. "You're a gorgeous girl, aren't you?" She wriggled in response, trying to lick my fingers.

"She sure is," Nash said, holding a French press, mugs, and a jug of milk on a tray. When a guy offers you coffee, you learn to expect instant, not real coffee in a French press. This guy had class.

He placed the tray on the coffee table in front of us and picked up one of the puppies himself. "This one I'm calling Clint, because he's such a tough guy."

I laughed. "He's too cute to be tough." The puppy on my lap wriggled off and promptly fell from the sofa and onto the floor. "Ooops!"

"She's all right," Nash said, leaning down and collecting her up himself. "See?" He turned her to face me, and my heart melted afresh.

"She has to be the cutest puppy on the planet. No offense, other puppies."

"I'm glad you like her. What would you like to call her?"

"I get to name her?"

"Well, hopefully we'll find a good home for her to go to and they'll name her, but until then, you can have the honors."

I reached for the puppy, and Nash handed her to me. As I held her close to my face, she tried to lick me, her tongue darting in and out. I said the first name that popped into my head. "Lucky. Her name is Lucky."

Nash turned the puppy so he was looking at her face. "Lucky, huh? Yeah, I can see that." He placed the newly named Lucky in the pen with her mom and then proceeded to pick the rest of the litter up to follow suit. He sat back down next to me and poured some coffee into the mugs. "Just milk, right?"

I nodded at him, smiling. He'd noticed I didn't have sugar in my coffee.

He handed me a mug and sat back, cradling his own in his hands. "Let's make a plan."

"For what?" I took a sip of my coffee.

"Your new singing career."

I almost choked. "My what?"

"Well, your singing debut, I should say."

I smiled, the knot in my belly at the thought of singing for an audience not quite as tight as it had been. "I'll have a chat to the Cozy Cottage girls tomorrow."

"That is a very good start."

I beamed at Nash over my coffee mug. Yes, Lucky was the name—for me and the dog.

CHAPTER 11

"$\mathcal{W}$hat's with Antoinette's new look?" Cassie asked as she tucked into her flourless raspberry and chocolate cake at the Cozy Cottage Café a few days later. It was a stormy day, and it was nice to be safely tucked inside the welcoming café as the wind whipped the rain up outside.

"I know, right?" I replied, my own mouth full of my favorite orange and almond syrup cake.

"Who's Antoinette?" Paige asked, appearing by our table, dressed in her Cozy Cottage red apron with white polka dots, her dark hair swept up into high ponytail.

"She's a new member of the sales team. She's taken to wearing, ah, rather conservative clothes to work, lately," Cassie explained tactfully.

"Yeah, like she ran away and joined a nunnery or something," I added, discarding Cassie's tact and saying it like it was.

Ever since Antoinette had first turned up in the office with her new look, she had been sporting a new and wonderful version of the same outfit each day: a baggy, full-length dress in a muted tone, flat nondescript shoes, and her hair pulled back in a severe bun. I had to hand it to the woman, she'd got an idea in her head and had run with it. The woman had commitment.

She had been just as attentive as she'd been at our meetings before this odd transformation, taking copious notes, asking questions, and complimenting me on everything from my presentations to my administration skills.

She was still a one-woman cheer team.

"Huh. I wonder why? Anyway, you haven't told us about your date with Nash, Marissa. That's what I want to hear about," Paige said with her eyebrows raised in expectation. "We need all the details, and fast; Bailey and I are swamped today. Sophie called in sick."

"Pull up a chair, then."

"I can give you precisely two minutes." Paige plunked herself down, and I launched straight into it, telling my friends about the picnic and the concert, about how Nash liked my "rain hair," and all the amazing kissing we had done on his sofa, surrounded by the dogs.

Once I had finished, I let out a contented sigh. It really had been an epic date.

"So, you're totally over the dog-slobber thing?" Cassie asked.

Dog Slobbergate felt a million years ago. "Absolutely."

"You really like this guy, don't you?" Paige asked, trying—and failing—to suppress an eager grin.

I shrugged, wanting to appear relaxed, while inside my heart rate kicked up a notch. "Yeah, he's pretty cool."

"'Pretty cool'? Just look at you, you're in love."

I scoffed. "Don't be ridiculous. I've only been out with him four times."

"That's enough," Cassie said. "When you know, you know. At least, that's how it was with me and Will. Am I right, Paige?"

Paige nodded, a goofy grin on her face. "Yeah, it's true. I always thought it was just something people said, but then, with Josh, I knew they were right. It felt . . . different."

"So?" Cassie led.

Was Cassie right? Was I in love with Nash? If I wasn't, I was well on my way to being so. I looked up at my friends' expectant faces. "I don't know. Maybe soon?"

Paige clapped her hands together. "Oh, the Last First Date Pact is weaving its magic once more. This is meant to be."

I shook my head. "Don't you have a café to run?"

Paige rolled her eyes. "Okay, we get the hint. We won't push you any further." She stood up and tucked her chair under the table. "Just, I want you to know I'm incredibly happy for you."

I grinned at her. They were right, it did feel different with Nash. It was calm, easy, as though we'd known each other our whole lives, when in reality it had only been a few weeks.

I knew I was all in, boots and all.

And I was pretty darn happy for myself, too.

* * *

TWO COFFEES, one slice of flourless raspberry and chocolate cake, and one slice of orange and almond syrup cake later, Cassie and I stood up to leave. As we headed to the door, we waved at Bailey and Paige, both working behind the counter, looking like a couple of glamorous TV chefs in their matching aprons.

"Actually, Cassie? Do you mind if you go back without me? I need to talk to Paige and Bailey about something."

With Nash's unstinting encouragement, I had decided today was the day: I was going to ask if I could sing at the café.

"That's very mysterious of you. Okay, see you back in the office. Remember, we've got that team catch-up at eleven."

With Cassie gone, I waited behind an older man who was taking his time deciding whether to have a slice of the rhubarb and strawberry pie or a slice of the carrot cake with cream cheese frosting. Eventually, his decision made—a slice of each—I had Bailey and Paige to myself for a moment.

"How are the Cozy Cottage Jams going?" I asked as my heart hammered in my chest.

"Oh, so great! We're selling out most sessions. Want to come this Friday? Hey, bring Nash! We'd love to meet him, right, Paige?" Bailey asked as she rearranged some sugar cookies on a plate by the cash register.

"Oh, yes! Great idea. The famous Nash, who Marissa may or may not be falling for," Paige teased, waggling her eyebrows at me.

I shook my head good-naturedly. "Sure, although that's not why I wanted to talk about it."

"Oh?" Bailey raised her eyebrows.

"I . . . ah, I wanted to ask you a favor." My hands began to sweat. Wow, I was nervous!

"Anything," Bailey replied.

I bit my lip. *Okay, here goes nothing.* "Can I perform one night? You know, just a song, maybe when you have someone else, too?"

"Really?" Paige asked with a surprised smile. "You have a beautiful voice, but I had no idea you wanted to perform." Paige had heard me sing at karaoke a few times, usually when we were a little trashed, which everyone knows is a prerequisite for karaoke singing.

"Really." I held my breath, awaiting their response.

I watched as Bailey and Paige shared a look. What did *that* mean? Was it a good look? Were they wondering how to let me down gently? I noticed Paige gave her a small nod.

Bailey turned to me. Her expression went from confused to happy. "Of course, you can! We could make it an open mic night. It'll be fun."

Paige put her hands to her mouth. "Oh, my gosh! This is going to be so amazing!"

My grin was as wide as my teenage jeans used to be. I leaned across the counter and gave them both an awkward hug. "Thanks, guys. I promise I won't let you down."

After bidding them farewell, I walked out of the café, a mixed bag of heightened emotions: excitement, trepidation, mind-crippling fear. But above all, proud of myself. I had taken the first step to overcoming my fears and doing something I'd always wanted to do.

And it was all because of Nash.

* * *

ON MY WAY TO work the following morning, I decided to share my exciting news with Nash in person. Knowing he started work early, I arrived at the building site with two take-out coffees at just before seven thirty. Putting the cups on the ground by my feet, I sent off a quick text, asking him what he was up to. I got one back almost immediately.

Working. Rather be with you. xx

After I'd stopped grinning for a full two minutes, I replied.

Come out to the sidewalk then. xx

Almost as soon as I'd slipped my phone back into my purse, Nash appeared from the side of the plastic-wrapped building. Wearing his hard hat, shorts, and work boots, he looked good enough to eat. He collected me up in a hug, and I breathed in his wonderful Nash scent.

"Hey, you," he said, still holding me close and giving me a kiss. I kissed him back, thankful the building was now enclosed so we didn't have an audience of gawping workmen.

"I wanted to give you this," I said, leaning down to pick up the coffee and handing it to him.

"Thank you."

"And, I have some news."

He took a sip of his coffee and waited.

"Bailey and Paige said I could perform at the café. They're having an open mic night soon."

"That's awesome!" He collected me up in another hug, lifting me off the ground and spinning me around.

"Your coffee!" I squealed, but loving his reaction nonetheless.

He placed me back on the sidewalk. "It's fine." He showed me his coffee cup, lid still on, with miraculously no spillage.

"You're a magician."

"I can handle my woman *and* my coffee," he said with a glint in his eye.

I chuckled. "That you can."

"So, when's the big performance?"

I pressed my lips together as the nerves jangled inside. "Not for a few weeks, so I have plenty of time to choose my song. I'm going to need to practice. Like, really practice."

"You're going to be great. Hey, let's go to a gig on Friday night to check it out."

"My friends will all be there," I replied uncertainly. Things seemed more serious when you met one another's friends.

"I'd like to meet them." Nash smiled at me.

There was a loud clanging sound emanating from the site, making me jump.

"I'd better go and check on that," Nash said, pulling me in for another kiss. "Thanks for the coffee and your news."

"You're welcome. On both counts."

He took a step away from me, turned, and said, "It's pretty cool to have a girlfriend who sings."

"A . . . a . . . girlfriend?" I stuttered as the air was sucked out of me. I blinked at him, my mind racing.

"Yeah. A girlfriend," Nash confirmed with a smile. His face changed when he took in my expression. He took a step closer to me. "Or not? Whatever. We don't have to label this." He put his hands on my arms. "Breathe, breathe."

I took a series of deep breaths, calming my nerves. It was one thing for me to begin to feel like Nash was the guy for me, it was quite another for him to say it out loud.

"Another freak-out?" Nash asked gently.

I nodded, not trusting my voice to speak, willing my heart rate to return to normal.

"You okay now?"

"I'm your girlfriend," I said with a small smile.

"If that's okay with you?" he asked uncertainly. "Just, I can't imagine wanting to date anyone else."

"Me neither," I almost whispered.

He nodded as a small smile crept across his face, our eyes locked. "Good."

"Good," I confirmed. "I would like that."

"To be my girlfriend?"

"Yes, to be your girlfriend."

We stood on the street, grinning at one another for a long moment until another loud crashing sound broke the spell. "I'll call you."

I watched him walk back into the plastic-wrapped building and took a moment to collect my thoughts. We were "official" boyfriend and girlfriend.

And it felt darn good.

CHAPTER 12

On Friday evening, I arrived home to Ryan in his usual spot, sprawled out on my lovely sofa, remote control in one hand, a beer in the other.

"Hey, Ryan," I said, keeping my tone light.

He glanced up at me and almost smiled. Either that or it was wind. "Hey, sis." He returned his attention to the screen.

I dropped my purse on the kitchen table and plunked myself down on the sofa next to him, ignoring the mild beer stench coming from his general direction. "How was your day?" I asked, scrunching up my face.

He let out a heavy sigh. "The usual."

I noticed he hadn't changed out of his work clothes, and his shirt was now a crinkled mess. Ryan worked as an architect at a small firm in the city. Up until Amelia walked out on him, he had been a happy, driven, career-oriented man with a bright future, designing houses and small buildings around the city. And now? Now it was like he had reverted to that morose teenager I remembered when I was twelve. This was not a good thing. Something needed to be done to pull him out of his reverie—and for me to get my home back.

"Work problems?"

Another sigh. "No, just . . . you know."

"Amelia?"

Yet another sigh. "Yeah. She's still with some guy; I'm still alone."

I bit my lip. He needed a change of subject to something less depressing. "Hey, so what are you up to tonight?"

"This." He indicated the TV.

Without a second's thought, I took the remote from his hand and flicked the TV off.

"Hey!" he protested. "You can't do that."

"Why not? It's my TV, and you're coming out with me."

"What? No, I don't want to."

"I don't care whether you want to or not, Ryan. Staying here is not an option."

He huffed and puffed about being a man and being responsible for his own destiny, or some such garbage.

I ignored him as I stood up and offered him my outstretched hand. "Come on, you. Get up, have a shower, throw on some clothes. We've got a gig to go to."

As Ryan begrudgingly showered and changed, I pulled on a tunic dress and retouched my makeup. Following the rained-off concert with Nash, I had let my hair go curlier than usual. Not it's full-on bird's nest look, but more natural than I usually wore it. And it felt good. Different, but good.

After some more cajoling and a drive in my car later, Ryan and I pulled into a park.

He peered out of the passenger window. "I'm not going to enjoy it."

I rolled my eyes for the umpteenth time since I got home. "You don't even know what we're doing."

"Well, it can't be any better than watching the game on TV," he harrumphed.

"You. Out," I instructed as I swung my door open and stepped onto the footpath.

Ryan did as commanded, letting out one of those heavy sighs he seemed to be perfecting. He stepped onto the sidewalk, and I straightened the shirt I had made him wear. "There. Now you look like an actual human being."

"Very funny, sis. Can you please tell me where we're headed?"

"Come with me."

We walked a block up the street together and rounded a corner onto a familiar road. A couple of hundred yards later, we arrived at the Cozy Cottage Café front door.

"We're going for coffee?" Ryan asked, looking confused.

"You can have coffee if you want, but we're here for the Cozy Cottage Jam session. Savannah Smith is playing, you know, we saw her at that bar last year?"

Ryan nodded at the memory, and I could have sworn I detected a hint of a smile. "Yeah, I remember. You brought that guy, what was his name? Henry or something."

"Harry." I pulled a face.

"What was wrong with him again?"

"I don't remember." Which was a total lie.

"Yeah, you do." Ryan was clearly not accepting my response.

I caved. "Okay. He had a weird pimple on the end of his nose."

He shook his head. "That's right. A pimple."

Wow, I had been so easily put off by the smallest thing. I had come a long, long way, baby. Not only was I on my fifth date with a guy tonight, but he was my *boyfriend*.

We pushed through the double doors into the busy café. There was a small stage with a microphone and chair where some tables sat during the day, and the place was already eighty percent full.

"Hi, Marissa!" Sophie said, grinning at me.

"Hey, Sophie." I returned her friendly smile. "Look, I'm meeting friends here but I need to see if you've got room for one extra."

Sophie glanced at Ryan and then back at me. "Cassie, Will, and Josh are already here." She nodded at a table at the back of the café, and I spotted my friends, chatting and laughing together. "We're pretty full tonight."

"Just one more? It's for my brother."

"You're Marissa's brother?" Sophie asked Ryan.

"Oh, I'm sorry. This is Ryan."

"Hey," Sophie replied, smiling at him, "It's great to meet you. You really look like your sister."

"You think?"

"Totally, only you're more manly and everything, of course." She smiled at him from under her lashes.

I widened my eyes. Was Sophie *flirting* with my brother?

"Thanks," Ryan replied with a laugh. "It's often good to be manly when you're, you know, a man."

I watched the interchange, wide-eyed. What was that on Ryan's face, a smile? My brother was *smiling*?

Sophie threw her head back and laughed at his comment.

I nudged Ryan in the arm. He shot me a look before returning his attention to Sophie. As I stood there like a third wheel while she continued to flirt with Ryan, I hoped it might spark something in him —because anything was better than watching him mooning over Amelia all day long.

"Yeah, and that's why I like to wear this shirt."

"Fascinating," Ryan replied.

I reached into my purse. "Here you go," I said to Sophie, handing over two tickets.

She took them in one hand and placed her other over her chest. "Oh, sorry! I totally forgot. Thanks. Take a seat. The extra ticket's on the house." She looked up through her lashes once more at Ryan. "Nice to meet you, Ryan."

"You too."

We made our way through the tables toward my friends at the back of the café. I began to rib Ryan.

"You are such a flirt."

"Me? It was all her. I was just the victim."

"Sure. A willing victim. Still, it was nice to see you happy for a change."

111

"I've been a bit of a drag, haven't I?"

I scrunched up my face. "Kinda?"

He shook his head and let out a puff of air. "It hit me hard."

I rubbed his arm. "I know. But we're here to listen to some music and have fun, so there will be no talking about She Who Shall Not Be Named, okay?"

"That sounds like a great plan." He smiled at me. "Do they serve beer here?"

"How about we stick to the Cokes tonight?" I suggested, remembering him as a recent maudlin drunk.

"Sure." He grinned at me, and it felt like I had my big brother back, the one I could hang out with, rely on, the one who hadn't had his heart ripped out of his chest and flambéed before his eyes.

"I'm interested to meet this boyfriend of yours. You haven't dated anyone seriously since—" He paused, looking up to the left as he thought.

"Eddie," I said for him. "Seven years ago."

"Seven years? Wow, that's a long time between drinks."

I spotted Bailey on the other side of the counter, handing some change over to a customer. I caught her eye and waved at her. We reached the table where Cassie greeted us enthusiastically. I introduced Ryan to Will and Josh, and they immediately began to bond in that male way guys do: talking about sports and how they were missing the big game tonight because they'd been dragged here instead.

"I think McConnell will smash it in the forwards tonight," Will said as the others nodded their heads.

Not having any idea who McConnell was and what he was going to smash, I took a seat next to Cassie, shrugging my jacket off and hanging it over the back of the chair.

"I am so excited to meet Nash," she said, her eyes shining.

"Not just spy on him from afar," I joked. "I'm a little nervous about it."

"Why?"

"What if you don't like him?"

"Honey, you do, and that's what matters."

"How about I go order us some Cokes?" Ryan offered, standing up.

"Sure. Get three. Nash will be here soon," I replied. "You guys want anything?" I asked the others.

"My girlfriend's getting ours," Josh replied with a smile. Josh and Paige had only been dating for a short time and were one hundred percent still in that "new flush of love" stage.

With Ryan at the counter, ordering our drinks, I took the time to look around the café. In a few short weeks, that would be my stool up there, my microphone. I tapped my foot on the hardwood floor. I had already begun to work out what I wanted to sing. I had learned how to play the guitar when I was a kid and still played from time to time. Now, it was time to get serious.

I looked over at the counter and spotted Ryan talking with Bailey. He looked even more animated than when he and Sophie were flirting. I shook my head. Perhaps all he needed was the chance to flirt with some good-looking women?

What was that saying? To get over someone you had to get under someone else? *Euw!* That was my brother! I didn't need to go thinking about that, even if it made me happy to see him happy for a change.

"Is this seat taken, miss?"

I dragged my eyes from Bailey and Ryan to see Nash's gorgeous face, grinning down at me. I stood up and wrapped my hands around his neck, planting a kiss on his lips.

"Now, if only I could get all the girls to greet me like that."

"Only me, thank you." I turned to face my friends' inquisitive faces. "Everyone, this is Nash."

Nash proceeded to shake hands with Cassie, Will, and Josh before taking a seat next to me. "So, I take it you're over the 'girlfriend' freak-out from before?" he asked in my ear.

"Well and truly."

We grinned at one another, and those hamsters started up their routine in my tummy once more.

"Oh, hey, man. You must be Nash," Ryan said as he stood before us, balancing three Cokes in his hands.

I plucked one out and placed it on the table. "Thank you, brother. Yes, this is Nash. Nash, Ryan."

The Cokes safely delivered to the table, the men shook hands. My best friends and my brother were meeting my boyfriend. There was something about it that made my heart swell.

Ryan took his seat next to Nash. "This place is full of beautiful women."

"Is it? I hadn't noticed," Nash replied, taking my hand in his under the table.

I shot him a smile. Looking back at Ryan, I said, "I saw you talking with Bailey."

"Is that her name? She's hot."

"Bailey is a fine-looking woman," Will said, and Cassie slapped him playfully on the arm. "What? She is objectively beautiful."

"She is," Josh chimed in.

"It's true," Cassie confirmed. "I don't get why she's still single."

"She's single, huh?" Ryan said, his interest piqued. He looked over at Bailey once more.

I shook my head at him. Although I didn't want to think about Ryan's love life, especially if it involved lusting after my close friends, it was nice to see him having a great time.

"Anyway, Bailey recommended we order dinner before the gig starts, so I got us a selection of those little tasting plate things."

"Tapas?" I offered.

"That's the one." Turning to Nash, Ryan said, "What do you do for a living?"

"I work in construction. I'm a site manager."

I listened as they chatted about their respective careers. With Ryan an architect, they found some common ground almost immediately.

Paige materialized at our table with a tray full of tapas. "Hi, Marissa. I didn't know you were here." She shot me a grin. "Right, I have bruschetta, meatballs—"

"Just throw them all on the table. We're going to share," Ryan interrupted.

"No problem."

Once Paige placed the tapas on the table, I introduced her to Nash. I loved the way he stood up to shake her hand in greeting. If this were the Old West, he'd be tipping his hat at her and calling her "ma'am."

"He is cute," Paige said quietly in my ear, shooting me a meaningful look.

I grinned back at her, my belly warm. "I know."

The audience began to clap as Savannah Smith walked onto the stage, dressed in a long, flowing dress, her brown hair curling around her shoulders. She greeted everyone, introducing herself, and launched into her first song. Although I didn't know it—she wasn't big enough to be on the radio yet—it was a soft, pretty ballad, the type of song I planned on singing myself.

We ate and chatted and listened to the music, having a wonderful time. Nash got on so well with everyone, which made my heart sing. Even Ryan seemed to be having a good time, and I was glad I'd dragged him off the sofa to come out with us.

With the music over, the food all gone, we decided to call it a night. As we prepared to leave, there were still a few tables of stragglers left in the café. We congratulated a tired looking Bailey and Paige on another successful Cozy Cottage Jam on our way out the door. I half expected Ryan to ask for Bailey's number, but he didn't, which was for the best; he still had a load more post-Amelia stuff to work through.

Out on the street, I rubbed my bare arms in the cool evening air. "My jacket! I must have left it on the chair."

"I'll get it for you," Nash said, making for the door.

"No, it's okay. I'll do it."

I pulled the door open and made my way through the café to our table. When I reached the table, my jacket was nowhere to be seen. I glanced around the other chairs, but no sign. I bent down to check under the table, nothing.

I straightened up, puzzled. I was certain I had hung it over the back of my chair when I arrived.

"Is this what you're looking for?" a voice behind me said.

I turned to look at the person behind me, saying, "Thank y—" I stopped. I couldn't say another word. My throat went dry, and my belly did a massive flip-flop.

It was my ex. The man who broke my heart into a thousand pieces. Eddie.

CHAPTER 13

"*E*ddie," I whispered, barely able to catch my breath.

"Hi, Marissa. You look great. It's good to see you." He smiled at me, and my mind was instantly awash with every memory, every feeling, from our time together. It was Eddie. *My* Eddie. The love of my life.

The man who had broken my heart.

I blinked at him. My heart hammered so fiercely, it threatened to burst out of my chest.

You know the first time you bump into your ex after you've broken up, and you want to look your best, with a hot new guy on your arm, everything in your life as it should be? Well, I was that person and this was my time. I had my career, I looked good, I had just spent the evening with my amazing friends, and I had Nash. It could not have been a more perfect storm in which to see him.

But in a flash, I was that sad and desperate girl he'd left all those years ago.

He extended his hand, offering me my jacket. I took it, mumbling my thanks, struggling to come to terms with the fact Eddie—*Eddie!*— was standing a mere three feet away. If I reached out, I could touch him, this man who had occupied my thoughts for so long.

I'd fallen into one of those weird Dali pictures with the melting clocks—only I was the one melting.

"What are you doing here?" I breathed, twisting the jacket in my hands.

"I came to see the gig. She was good."

He had been here all evening?

He looked casually around the café, as though his throat hadn't seized up and his mind wasn't racing a mile a minute. And, perhaps, it wasn't.

"This is a great place. I've never been here before."

"Um, yeah."

"It's good to see you," he repeated and smiled again.

"You . . . you said that." I couldn't tear my eyes away from his handsome face. I would love to say he looked terrible, that he'd lost his hair, put on ten or fifty pounds, perhaps even lost a few of his teeth. But he hadn't. His dark hair was cropped shorter than it used to be, but his eyes were just as green, his body just as long and lean, suggesting he still worked out, still took good care of himself.

He looked like the same old Eddie, the Eddie who could make my heart sing, the Eddie I had loved with all my heart.

Damn him to darnation!

"Do you have a minute? I saw you were here with friends, so maybe you need to go back to them, only I'd like to talk."

"Friends, yes. I was here with friends." I thought of Nash, waiting patiently for me outside the café, and was forced to swallow my guilt. Why hadn't I mentioned my boyfriend? Wasn't that the general idea when you saw your ex? Rub in how incredibly happy you were and how him leaving you was really the best thing to ever happen?

He took a step closer to me. "If you have to go, maybe we could meet up tomorrow? I would really like that."

"Tomorrow?" I let out a puff of air. Eddie wanted to see me tomorrow? "Oh, tomorrow. Yes, well, I have a thing, and then another . . . thing. So, sorry . . . I can't."

He looked utterly crestfallen. I wanted to wrap him up in a comforting embrace and kiss away his worries, tell him I was wrong, that I would do whatever he wanted. But I didn't. I couldn't. Seeing him was so unexpected, so totally derailing.

I locked my jaw, determined not to let him get to me. I had come too far. Hadn't I?

"Okay. I get it. I was terrible to you, horrible. You didn't deserve it."

I nodded. *Good summation.*

"Marissa, you have to believe me when I say, not a day has gone by since we broke up when I haven't felt like the total piece of dirt I was."

I swallowed, bit my lip. Where was this going?

"And, well, seeing you here tonight reminded me how great those days were."

I narrowed my eyes at him. These were the words I had wanted to hear for so long.

"They were great." I glanced at the door. "Look, Eddie, it's been so," —gut-wrenching, confusing, off-the-charts insane?—"*unexpected* to see you. In a good way, of course. But . . . I really have to go."

"I get it." He nodded, looking forlorn once more. "I'll see you around. Take good care, okay?"

I nodded back at him. "Thanks, I will." With my jacket in my hands, on shaking legs, I walked toward the door.

As I passed him, he reached out and lightly held onto my arm, looking intently at me. "I . . . it was good to see you," he said quietly.

I looked down at this hand on my bare arm and then back up into his eyes.

"See you later, Marissa!" Paige called from behind the counter, bringing me to my senses.

I barely registered her as I pushed my way through the door and stumbled out of the café. I could still feel Eddie's hand on my arm, hear his words ringing through my head. I took a deep, gasping breath, the world a blur around me as I tried to steady myself.

"Are you all right?" Nash asked, his hand on my back.

I looked up into his face, etched with concern. "Yes, yes, I'm fine. Sorry."

Why was I apologizing?

"Are you sure? You look like you've seen a ghost."

I shot him a surprised look. I had seen a ghost, one that had thrown me into a tailspin.

"Hey, you two lovebirds," Cassie teased. "We're calling it a night. See you on Monday, okay?" She gave me a quick hug, and I had to remind myself to hug her back. "It was so awesome meeting you, Nash." I watched in a daze as she hugged Nash, too.

"Yeah, good to meet you, mate," Will said, pumping Nash's hand.

I watched as though through a camera lens as Nash and Josh also shook hands, bidding one another farewell. Then, it was Ryan's turn. It was all happening around me, but I didn't feel part of it. All I could think about was Eddie. Eddie turning up at my favorite place. Eddie saying he'd treated me badly and felt terrible about it.

Eddie wanting to see me again.

"Marissa?"

I came back to reality to see Ryan shooting me a quizzical look.

"Did you hear me?"

"Sorry, what?" I tried to focus on his face.

"I said, I can hitch I ride with Josh, if you like? He's offered to take me home."

I glanced at Nash and back at Ryan. "I . . ." What did I want? I was too confused. Part of me wanted to curl up on Nash's sofa, eat chocolate, and enjoy the feeling of being safe, of being with a man who liked me, who was uncomplicated, who was new.

Another part of me wanted to storm back into the café and confront Eddie over what he did to me and . . . and, what?

And kiss him?

"You okay, sis?" Ryan asked, his head cocked to the side.

Finding some form of inner strength, I replied, "Actually, I'm not feeling that well, so I think I might just head home." I turned to Nash. "Is that okay? I'm so sorry, I have a headache coming on."

Not the most original excuse known to womankind, but it was all I could think of at the time and I was running with it.

"Of course," he said softly. Not for the first time tonight, I swallowed my guilt. He pulled me in for a hug, and I breathed in his comforting scent. "I'll call you tomorrow."

I nodded and smiled, tears threatening my eyes. Tomorrow. Yes. Tomorrow things would feel different, tomorrow things would make sense. Tomorrow I could see Eddie's words as what they were: an apology, an apology I needed to accept and move on from

Tomorrow, everything would be clear.

* * *

ONLY, it wasn't. It was far from clear.

I woke up in twisted sheets, feeling as though I hadn't slept a wink. My mind was full to bursting, cycling through my conversation with Eddie and trying to work out the meaning behind what he'd said.

Why did he want to see me? He had looked so hurt when I had said no to him. What did it mean?

In an instant, I was a young eighteen-year-old once more, back when Eddie was mine. I let out a sigh, full of longing. The way he would look at me, the love in his eyes, the warmth in his smile. He had made me feel like I was all that mattered to him, like his life held no meaning without me.

And we had been good together. We would go on early morning runs, preparing ourselves mentally and physically for the day. Although we were students and had next to no money, he would take me to romantic places, pick wild flowers for me, surprise me with a romantic picnic for two at our favorite beach. It was magical time, a time I had found so hard to forget.

I glanced at the clock on my nightstand: nine thirty. Wow, I had overslept! That wasn't like me in the least.

I threw my covers off and swung my legs over the side of the bed, sitting upright and running my hands through my hair. I locked my jaw. Part of me screamed, "How dare he do this to me!" Just when my life was going great, he had to turn up and remind me of the person I once was, before I was "Marissa Jones, successful career woman," with my own apartment and life.

And Nash.

I scrunched my eyes shut. *Nash.* He was amazing, everything I could want in a man. My freak-outs didn't faze him in the least, he was kind and sweet, heart-stoppingly handsome, quite possibly the best kisser on the planet, and the man packed a good picnic. All in all, he was perfect.

But he wasn't Eddie.

I let out a heavy sigh. I stood up and padded down the hallway to the kitchen. Perhaps coffee could help me out of my malaise?

"Hey," Ryan grunted from his habitual spot on the sofa. "Your headache any better?"

"Headache? Oh, yeah. It's better, thanks." I pulled a tub of coffee out of the pantry and proceeded to make myself a cup. "Want one?" I offered Ryan.

"Sure."

With the coffee made, we sat in silence, side-by-side on my sofa, nursing our respective mugs. Some cop show I don't watch on TV was set to mute.

"Nash seems nice," Ryan said, his eyes on the screen, his words punctuating the silence.

"Yes. Yes, he is," I replied.

He was right, Nash was nice. *So* nice. He had got on so well with everyone, laughing and talking about anything and everything. I'd felt so close to him, all evening, stealing glances at one another, not being able to stop smiling when our eyes had met.

I was sure he was the guy for me.

Or, at least, I was sure he was, until I saw Eddie.

"You seeing him today?" Ryan asked, taking a sip of his coffee. "Ah, that hits the spot."

I thought about our plans. Before my "headache," we had agreed to meet at his place so I could see Lucky and the puppies, then head out to the dog park with Dex, the one we had gone to on our first ever date. Nash had joked it would be a "reclamation of the space," imitating those hipster types with the ironic man buns who liked to talk in that pretentious way. It had been funny at the time.

Now? Not so much.

I bit my lip. "I'm meant to see him, yes," I replied.

THREE LAST FIRST DATES

"Mind if I turn this back up? It's getting to the good part." Ryan scooped up the remote lying on the cushion between us.

I shrugged. "Sure." I had no interest in watching cops chase baddies, but anything was better than the inner turmoil currently duking it out in my brain.

"Oh, your phone's been beeping like mad this morning," Ryan said, nodding at my phone, sitting on the coffee table in front of me.

I reached out and picked it up. There were messages from Cassie and Paige and Bailey, all raving about Nash: how charming he was, how good-looking he was, how nice he was. Paige waxed lyrical over no less than seven messages about how she simply knew he was The One for me and how lucky I was to have found him.

I let out a heavy sigh. They were right, all of them. Nash was amazing, and I was incredibly lucky to have him. So, why did I feel like this?

My phone beeped in my hand once more. Expecting another message extoling Nash's perfection, I glanced at the screen. My heart stopped.

I need to see you.

It was from Eddie.

My mind began to race. What did he mean? Why did he *need* to see me, not just *want* to see me? Did he want to apologize again? Maybe he was doing some sort of twelve-step program to become a better human being or something? I could be one of those people he needed to apologize to, to make recompense.

I scrunched my eyes shut, then opened them again to look at the screen. *Yup, message still there, still from Eddie.*

There had to be an explanation for this. The cogs in my brain continued to whir.

Was the message meant for me, or was his fiancée also called Marissa, by some weird cosmic coincidence?

Okay, so I realized that one was probably a long shot, but I was open to all possibilities.

With trembling fingers, I typed a one-word message back.

Why?

I held my breath, not taking my eyes from my screen. When his message arrived, the beep made me almost levitate off the sofa.

Because I can't stop thinking about you.

My breath hitched in my throat. Okay, so that was no twelve-step program.

I typed out a quick reply, my finger hovering over the "send" button for a moment. I pressed it, chewing my lip.

You're engaged.

My phone pinged once more.

Not anymore.

What?!

My eyes almost popped out of my head. Eddie was no longer engaged? When had that happened? With fingers I could barely control, I opened up my Facebook app and typed in his name, misspelling it several times in the process. Finally, I found it. Relationship status, where was relationship status? Bingo.

Single.

Oh, my gosh. I slumped back on the sofa, letting out a breath I hadn't realized I was holding. Eddie was single?

Ryan laughed, pulling me back to reality. "This guy is freakin' stupid if he can't see who the killer is," he commented, shaking his head.

"Yeah," I replied, not knowing who the "freakin' stupid" guy was, but happy, for once, Ryan was preoccupied with the TV.

I glanced at the large carriage clock on the wall. I needed to shower and get ready to leave. I had another date with Nash, perfect, wonderful Nash.

And I needed to push Eddie and his single-slash-engaged-slash-completely confusing status as far from my mind as was humanly possible.

CHAPTER 14

I arrived at Nash's place at eleven, as arranged. I would have loved to have been able to say I had conquered my inner turmoil, but I had only managed to park my conflicting feelings about Eddie to the back of my mind, where they had begun to fester like smelly food left in the refrigerator too long.

Try as I might, I couldn't forget the fact Eddie had called off his engagement. When did that happen? Was it before or after we bumped into one another last night? And if it was after, did I have anything to do with it? Did he do it for me?

I stood on Nash's doorstep and tried to collect my thoughts. I needed to focus on the present, not the past. Nash was my present; Eddie was my past. He wasn't relevant to me anymore.

"Hey, beautiful," Nash said as he opened the door. "You look amazing." He pulled me in for an embrace, kissing me on the lips.

I breathed in his scent, reminding myself how wonderful he was, and how, together, we had conquered my commitment-phobia. That *had* to mean something: something big, something important, something real.

Didn't it?

We followed the usual routine of closing the front door before opening the door to the living room. We didn't want any puppy escapees, and the pups had grown in ability and confidence since I first met them. As Nash swung the door open, I prepared to be mobbed—and mobbed I most certainly was. I crouched on the floor, the puppies treating me like a jungle gym, crawling all over me, licking me, their enthusiasm radiating out of their canine paws.

"You're a hit," Nash commented, smiling down at the six of us on the floor.

I stood back up, scooping Lucky up in my arms. She licked my neck with an enthusiasm I would love to feel today, making it tingle. She was warm and fluffy, and I couldn't help but clutch her against my chest, enjoying our uncomplicated closeness.

Gretel, the puppies' mom, nuzzled me, her tail wagging, and I patted her on the head. She looked so much healthier now. Nash had done a great job caring for her and her puppies.

"Do you want to play with the pups for a while? I'll go get Dexter ready to go to the park."

I tore my attention away from the lick-y, wriggly fur ball in my hands and looked at Nash. He was wearing his habitual shorts and T-shirt, a cap atop his head. My heart contracted as I looked into his smiling blue eyes. I smiled back at him. "Sure."

I sat back down on the hardwood floor, playing with the puppies. Two of them took the opportunity to investigate their surroundings further, but Lucky stuck by me. I stroked her fur from her head to her tail. "You don't have ex-boyfriend problems, do you?" I asked her quietly. She licked my hand in response, and I smiled at her. "No, you don't. You're the sensible one."

A moment later, Nash walked into the room with Dexter on a lead. His tail whacked against the side of the armchair as he spotted me with the puppies, their mom still by my side.

"Shall we head off? We can leave the pups in here with Gretel now. I've removed any stray slippers," Nash said with a chuckle.

"Sure." I looked back down at Lucky. There was something about being here with her uncomplicated affection I was reluctant to leave. I picked Lucky up and gave her a light kiss atop her head, leaving a dash of lipstick. "Oh, Lucky. That won't do at all." I rubbed it off with my fingers as best I could before placing her back on the floor with the other puppies and her mom.

I pushed myself up off the floor and brushed my jeans down, ridding them of only about half the fluff the dogs had deposited there. I didn't care in the least. I would have stayed here with them all day, if I could.

The puppies safely enclosed in the living room, Nash locked the door to the house and we walked down the driveway to his truck. As he opened the car for Dexter to jump in, I pulled my phone out of my purse. I had told myself I wouldn't check my phone.

After the conversation Eddie and I had had earlier, it was nothing short of date suicide.

Call it a lack of adult judgment, my commitment-phobia rearing its ugly head, or just plain old-fashioned curiosity, but something told me to check my phone. As I flipped it over in my hand I saw it, the words I'd wanted from Eddie for seven years:

I made a mistake.

I blinked at the screen as another message flashed up.

I'm at our place. Meet me there. Please.

In an instant, I was back at the beach we used to go to when we were together, a beach I had never been able to return to since. That beach was the place we had first kissed, the place we had first said those three little magic, wonderful words to one another. Asking me to meet him there could only mean one thing.

He was still in love with me.

I clutched onto my phone, watching Nash opening his door. He looked over at me, his face crinkling in concern when he took in my face.

"Marissa?" A few short steps with his long legs and he was by my side. "You've gone pale."

"I . . . I . . ." I stuttered. I looked down at the words on my phone, my heart thudding so loudly I was surprised Nash couldn't hear it.

"Is it your headache? Do you need to lie down? How about a glass of water?"

Nash was trying his best to help me, but I was barely taking his words in. I knew he couldn't help me. I knew that deep, deep down.

I looked up at him, resolved. "I have to go."

"Can I drive you?" he offered, rubbing my arms.

A pang of guilt hit me, right in the chest. "No, I . . . I think it's my headache. I can drive. I'll—" What? I'll do what? "I'll call you later," I managed as I took a step back from him, the lie sitting uncomfortably on my lips.

"As long as you're sure," Nash replied.

I forced a smile, my belly twisting. "Yes. Look, I'm sorry about this. I will call you when I'm . . . ah, feeling better."

Without looking up into his eyes, I turned on my heel and walked the few paces to my car. I didn't know what I was doing, but I knew I couldn't be here with Nash. Not after Eddie's words, not knowing he was no longer engaged. Not knowing he wanted to meet me in our special place. I had to know what it meant. I had to see him.

Without a backward glance, I started my car and pulled out, heading to the beach I once knew and loved.

And to the man I had never stopped loving.

* * *

AFTER GRIPPING the steering wheel so hard I was surprised I didn't snap it in two, I pulled into the gravel park next to our old beach. The traffic over the bridge north had been light enough that I made it there in only thirty-five minutes, enough time to run through every possible scenario in my head.

I climbed out of my car, slipped off my sneakers, and walked across the golden sand of the small beach, my heart in my mouth.

I spotted Eddie sitting, looking out at the sea, his arms wrapped around his knees. His shirt was pulled taut across his strong, muscular back, his shoes dropped casually at his side.

My breathing short and shallow, I took slow, deliberate steps toward him, until I was only a few feet away.

As though sensing my presence, he turned around and looked

directly at me with such longing, I swear my heart stopped. In one, swift moment, he was up on his feet, covering the short distance between us as I stood, rooted to the spot.

"Marissa," is all he said, his intense green eyes the color of the sea.

He reached out to me and I recoiled. I wasn't ready to be touched by him. Not yet. Maybe, not ever.

His handsome face creased into an uncertain smile. "I'm so glad you came."

I nodded at him, biting my lip. I didn't trust myself to speak. I barely knew what I was doing here, with him, in this place.

I needed to hear what he had to say.

Luckily, I didn't need to wait for long.

"Marissa, I need you to know something."

I looked intently at him, holding my breath, my hands clenched at my sides.

"It's you, Marissa. It's always been you."

"Wha—what are you saying?" I breathed, scarcely believing his words.

He took my cold hand in his. Although my body stiffened at his touch, I loosened my hand out, allowing his hand to warm mine. "I'm saying, I'm still in love with you."

My eyes grew to the size of saucers. "You're what?"

He grinned at me, as though what he was saying was the best news in the world. "I'm still in love with you, Marissa. Without even knowing I was doing it, I have compared every woman I've dated since we broke up to you and they—"

"Since you *left* me," I corrected, interrupting him, the memory smarting like a collective wasp sting.

He hung his head. "Yeah. Since I left you." Looking up at me again, he added, "Something I've regretted every day. Marissa, don't you see? Those other women came up short. It's you. You're The One." His eyes shone, his face beaming.

I, on the other hand, was reeling, my legs rendered virtually inoperable. I regarded him, slack-jawed, trying to take in what he was telling me. *He loved me. He'd always loved me. He regretted leaving me. I was The One.*

I had wanted to hear him say he had made a mistake, that he should never have left me, that I was the love of his life, for so many long, long years. And now, he was finally saying it, standing on the beach, in the very spot he had first professed his love for me all those years ago.

Finally, I had what I had wanted.

"Wh-what happened to your fiancée?"

"She's gone. It had been over for a long time, just neither of us had admitted it. And then, seeing you? Marissa, I knew I had to be with you. So, I called it off."

My hand flew to my chest. *He left his fiancée for me?*

"You called off your engagement for . . . for me?"

"Yes." His smile reached his eyes, lighting up his face, bringing back a flood of memories: the good times, the happy times, when we were in love and life felt full of possibilities.

"But . . . this wasn't just a girlfriend. You were going to get *married.*"

He let out a puff of air, shifting his hand in mine. "She wasn't right for me. It took seeing you for me to realize that. You, Marissa, wonderful, perfect you."

My heart expanded. *Wonderful, perfect me.*

"So?" He questioned when I remained silent, standing there, goggling him like a stunned fish. "What do you say?"

My heart pounded as I thought of Nash—kind, fun, sweet, gorgeous Nash. I was convinced he was the guy for me, that together, we could make it.

I looked up into Eddie's eyes. They were full of hope—and love.

In that moment, everything I had ever felt for him washed over me, lifting me up, making me see what I had been missing. The way he'd helped me grow, helped me become a woman. The way he'd made me feel so loved, so important.

He was my first love, the one I couldn't forget. No one had come close to him.

No one had had the chance.

"I say, yes." A smile teased the edges of my mouth until it was a full-blown, cheesy grin, spreading from ear to ear, the happiness threatening to spill right out of me.

"Really?" Eddie asked, his face alight with hope.

"Really." I stepped into him, and he wrapped his arms around me in an embrace. When his lips touched mine, my heart felt as though it might explode.

He picked me up and spun me around as we both laughed, giddy in our rekindled love.

Being back in Eddie's arms was everything I had ever wanted. And this time, it was going to stick. This time, we were going to be together forever.

CHAPTER 15

"*N*ash is such a nice guy," Bailey said on Monday morning when I dropped into the Cozy Cottage Café to get a take-out coffee on my way back from a customer meeting with Antoinette.

"Yes, he is," I replied, noncommittally.

I had yet to tell my friends about recent developments, and I was as nervous as a long-tailed cat in a room of rocking chairs to do so. I knew they wouldn't be happy with me, despite the fact I had found the perfect guy. It's just it wasn't Nash.

"I'm so pleased you chose him. Not that I know what the other guys were like, of course, but it's hard to imagine they could be better," Bailey continued as I paid for a coffee for me and an orange juice for Antoinette, "or as cute," she added with raised eyebrows.

I smiled weakly at her. "How was your weekend?" I asked, choosing to change the subject instead.

As she told me about working on Saturday and what movie she'd seen, my mind wandered back to where it had firmly been for the last forty-eight hours: Eddie. He and I had spent the rest of the weekend together. It had been everything I had hoped for. It had been pure bliss.

I let out a contented sigh. "You've got it bad," Bailey commented, grinning at me.

"What? Oh, I was just thinking about work," I lied, a knot forming in my belly.

"Is that what you're calling Nash, is it?" Bailey replied with a wink. "Got it."

I cleared my throat. Although I knew I would eventually need to tell my friends about the redirection of my affections, I didn't want to do it today, especially not in front of Antoinette.

"Oh, and I have a date for the Cozy Cottage Jam open mic night, Friday, the twenty-fifth."

"That's only four weeks away!" I could feel the blood draining away from my face, a knot forming in my belly. Four weeks!

"I know. It's not long. What I'll do is give you the first slot of the night and then open it up to others. Did you want to do one or two songs?"

Antoinette ended her call and came to collect her orange juice. I glanced nervously at her.

"Oh, I had thought maybe just one?"

"Great. I'll put you down to sing one. Paige is in charge of the advertising on social media and the website, and she's already posted stuff, so I'm hoping for a good crowd."

"Are you singing here?" Antoinette asked, her eyebrows raised in surprise.

"Yes, I am." I smiled weakly at her, trying to feel positive about it.

My mind instantly darted to Nash. He was the one who had encouraged me to pursue my passion and sing. Now that I was with Eddie, he would miss my performance—as nice a guy as Nash was, I seriously doubted he'd want to come and see me sing after the conversation I planned on having with him later today.

A fresh pang of guilt hit me squarely in the gut.

Nash had sent me several messages over the weekend, checking in to see how I was feeling, offering to bring me chicken soup if I were still ill. I ignored them all, not knowing what to say to him now that I was back together with Eddie. I mean, I could hardly knock on his door and say, "Hey, Nash. Thanks for everything, but you're dumped because I got a better offer from a guy I've been in love with since I was eighteen."

Yeah, I wasn't looking forward to that conversation.

"Here you are," Sophie said, handing me my cup of take-out coffee. "I can't wait to hear you sing."

"Me too," Antoinette echoed.

I flashed them both a nervous smile as I took the coffee from Sophie. "I'm not sure if I'll be any good, but I figured I'd give it a shot."

"Good for you," Sophie said with a warm smile. "Do you know what you're going to sing?"

"'Thinking Out Loud,'" I replied automatically, naming one of my favorite shower songs. In there, it sounded amazing. Would it here, in a roomful of people, all watching me, listening to every word I sang? I swallowed, the knot tightening in my belly.

"Oh, I love that song!" Sophie said. "I can't wait."

"Me, neither," Antoinette said, collecting her bottle of juice from the counter. "Especially since this is your first time."

I shot her a quizzical look.

"I mean, so that we can all support you," she added hastily.

As we turned to leave, Paige came out from the kitchen, a tray of sliced cakes in her hands. "Hi, Marissa." She had a huge smile on her face as she placed the tray on the counter in front of me. "Nash is spectacular! I'm so happy for you!"

Again, the guilt twisted inside. "He is." I plastered on a fake smile, hoping my sweet friend wouldn't notice. Nash was going to be so upset with me. I glanced down at the cakes. "Can I get a slice of the chocolate cake to go?"

"Not your usual?" Paige shot me a questioning look.

"Ah, no. I feel like a change today." I shifted uncomfortably.

"Sure." She picked up a slice and slipped it into a brown paper bag.

"I've never met a slice of Cozy Cottage cake I didn't want to eat."

"Here. On the house." She handed me a slice.

I took the bag from her. "What's that for?"

She shrugged, glancing at Bailey.

134

"We have a feeling about you two," Bailey said. Standing next to Paige, both dressed in their fifties-inspired dresses and Cozy Cottage Café aprons, they looked like a couple of beautiful sisters from *Peyton Place*.

Again with the guilt. I decided to deflect. "Thank you both. Look, Antoinette and I need to get going. We're meeting with a big customer. See you both later."

I turned and left without a backward glance, feeling their eyes boring holes in my back. I would tell them about Eddie soon enough, and they would be happy for me—eventually.

We drove the short distance to Pukeko Chocolates where we met a nervous Bryce, my favorite tech guy, at the front of the building.

"I just saw Steve Bryant leave," he said, his eyebrows drawn together.

"Oh," I replied, biting my lip. "That's not good."

"Who's Steve Bryant?" Antoinette asked, her eyes darting between Bryce and me.

"He's Telco's top sales person. And he was with that asshole, Mark Watson."

"Who's Mark Watson?"

"Only the worst person to walk the face of the earth," Bryce replied, his jaw set.

I couldn't help but chuckle. It was a little extreme, particularly for the mild-mannered Bryce. "Really?"

"Really." Bryce's nostrils flared, and I realized this was no joking matter.

"That sounds like a story," I said.

"A story of betrayal." Bryce's face was grim.

"What did he do?" Antoinette asked, as riveted as I was.

"Let's just say, winning this business just got personal," Bryce replied, looking off into the distance like he was in some cheesy action movie.

"Wow. Pretty serious."

"If you call stealing my girlfriend and ruining my life serious, then yeah, this is serious."

Although I had met Steve Bryant at several industry events, where he never failed to boast about his latest success while making my eyes water with his heavy cologne, I had no clue who Mark Watson was. But, in solidarity with Bryce, I already loathed him.

"Shall we do this?" I asked.

Bryce narrowed his eyes, squaring his narrow shoulders. "Oh, yes. Let's do this."

Like a trio of action heroes, intent on revenge—and to win some new business—we walked through the automatic glass doors into Pukeko Chocolates' white, gleaming reception. With me in my typical pencil skirt and blouse combo, five foot five Bryce in his "I spend too much time gaming to bother with fashion" geek clothes and open-toed sandals, and Antoinette still imitating the Amish, we looked more like we were from a comedy than an action movie. But we were resolute, and we knew we had what it took.

We knew we needed to win this business for Bryce now. And we were determined to do it.

* * *

An hour and a half later, we reached the AGD offices and I went straight to Cassie's office. She was on a call, but when she saw me, standing in her office doorway, she quickly ended it.

"How did it go?" she asked, standing up and walking around her desk.

"It went well." I could feel the excitement rising inside.

"How well?" Cassie asked, her eyes narrowed.

"We don't officially know yet because they told us they need to meet to discuss the shortlisted proposals."

"Us and Telco?"

I nodded, pressing my lips together. "Steve Bryant."

"Damn it!" Cassie replied, echoing my very thought when we'd seen him outside the customer earlier. She let out a puff of air. "Well, I suppose we can hope that gallon of aftershave he likes to wear gave them all allergies or something."

I grinned at her. "I haven't told you what happened next."

Cassie's face lit up. "What happened?"

"Well, after we had shaken hands and agreed they would come back to us in the next few days with a decision, Don Ackerman tracked us down at reception."

"Don's the head of purchasing, right?"

"Right. Anyway, it turns out he's a family friend of Antoinette's, and he told us—unofficially, of course—that we were easily the front-runners for their business." I beamed at Cassie, my excitement threatening to overflow.

Cassie put her hand over her mouth, her eyes gleaming. "Go Antoinette's family friend!"

"Cassie, I don't want to get ahead of myself," I said, totally getting ahead of myself, "but I think this one may be in the bag."

Cassie returned my smile. "Great work, Marissa."

I left Cassie's office and floated back to my desk. Everything was coming together for me: bringing in a major new client, finally pursuing my singing passion, and Eddie coming back to me. My heart contracted at the thought of him. He had said the right words at the right time, and I had fallen straight back in love with him.

* * *

AFTER SUCH A SUCCESSFUL morning at work, I was brought back down to earth with a *thud* when I met Nash for "the dreaded talk." I knew I could have broken up with him over text, but he was too great a guy to do that to. So, I decided to "woman up" and do it in person. And I was *not* looking forward to it.

I had replied to his texts late on Sunday night, pleading a weekend of illness, and agreed to meet for a quick drink after work at O'Dowd's.

I was as nervous as a turkey at Christmas when I walked through the door and into the dimly lit bar. I spotted Nash, standing with his back to me, talking with Buff behind the bar. I was instantly taken back to one of the Three Last First Dates I had in this very place, with

Blaze, the protein-mad bodybuilding menswear shop assistant. I shook my head at the memory. That felt so long ago.

I watched Nash for a moment, plucking up my nerve. I had kept my contact with him light and breezy. For all he knew, we were meeting for a girlfriend-boyfriend drink. I chewed the inside of my lip. I was about to totally wreck his day.

With my nerves clanging, I walked over and stood next to him. As he turned to face me, my breath caught in my throat. Why did he have to have the sort of lips I wanted to kiss and kiss until my own lips were bruised? He smiled at me, and a bunch of Boy Scouts tightened the already large knot inside.

"Hey, beautiful," he said, using the nickname he had begun to use for me. He slipped his arm around my waist and planted a slow and sexy kiss on my lips.

I closed my eyes, lost in it. I was powerless to resist. His scent, his touch, the way his arm felt through the fine fabric of my blouse. Everything about the way he kissed me was absolutely perfect. There was something about Nash I found irresistible. Well, almost.

Eddie. I had to think about Eddie.

I pulled away from him and glanced at the two Cokes sitting on the bar. "Is one of those for me?"

"Sure is. Let's go and sit." He picked the drinks up and began to walk toward the booth at the back of the bar where I had sat with Blaze, those few short weeks ago.

"How about here?" I suggested as we walked past a barrel with a handful of stools encircling it.

Nash shrugged. "Sure." He put the drinks on the barrel table, and we sat down. "It's great to see you looking better. The headache's all gone?"

"Mm-hm." I tried my best to appear normal, as though I hadn't been lying to him all weekend and I wasn't about to drop a bombshell on him when he least expected it. Behind the table, I clasped my hands.

"Fantastic." He reached for one of my hands, and I let him pull it in toward himself. "How was your day?"

I thought of the successful meeting I'd had with Pukeko Choco-lates. I wanted to tell him all about it, to listen to his encouragement, but I knew I needed to get this over with—for his sake, as well as for my own.

"Nash, I—" I began. The skin around his eyes crinkled in a smile, and I was forced to look down at the table. "I have to tell you something."

"What is it?"

I swallowed, my throat dry. I reached for my Coke and took a large sip, the bubbles climbing up into my nose, making my eyes water.

Nash chuckled. "You drank that too fast, didn't you?" he said gently as he reached out to put his hand on my cheek.

I put my hand on his and lowered it to the table. I pressed my lips together. "Nash, I need to say something."

He furrowed his brow. "It's not another freak-out, is it? Marissa, I told you, we can handle those."

"No, it's not. And I'm really sorry." I looked up at him as real tears stung my eyes. This was hard, so much harder than I thought it would have been.

He retreated from me, leaning away on his stool. "You're breaking up with me." It was a statement, not a question.

I nodded, holding my breath. "I'm sorry."

His jaw locked—only serving to make him look even more like the stoic Jon Snow—he pulled his hand away from me. "Why?"

I chewed the inside of my lip, my heart actually aching. "My boyfriend from a long time ago. He came back to me."

"When?"

"I saw him at the weekend."

"Was he your 'headache'?" he asked, his fingers in the air doing air quotes.

I gave a slow nod. Lying to Nash was the last thing I had wanted to do.

"I see."

I looked up at his face and then immediately looked down, a stab

139

of hurt cutting through me. He glared back at me, and if I could have, I would have shriveled up and disappeared from his sight.

He stood up, the stool falling behind him onto the hard floor, landing with a *clang*.

I could feel his eyes on me. I knew he was angry. I knew I had hurt him.

"I'm so sorry," I breathed, stealing a look at him.

He nodded, his lips—the lips I had kissed only moments ago—pressed into a thin line. "Me too."

I watched, barely able to breathe, as he turned his back to me, stepped over the fallen barstool, and stomped out of the bar, the door *swooshing* shut behind him. I sat still, rooted to my spot, my heart slamming against my chest.

Part of me wanted to run after him, fall to my knees, and beg him to forgive me, to forget what I had said, asking him to stay with me. And then I thought of Eddie and I knew, despite the hurt, the pain, I had done the right thing, the only thing.

As if activated by some cosmic force, my phone began to ring in my purse. In a daze, I reached in and pulled it out, seeing the name "Eddie" appear on the screen.

"Hey," I said into the receiver.

"Hi. Have you done it?"

At the sound of Eddie's voice, my face creased up and the tears flowed. "Yes," I replied, my voice quavering.

In the interest of full-disclosure, I had told Eddie about Nash. He had been upset I was involved with someone else and had asked me to end it as soon as possible, which is what I had done.

"Good. Come over to see me."

"Okay." I hung up and took another sip of my Coke.

What was done was done. I knew it was for the best, even if my heart felt like it was breaking in two.

CHAPTER 16

I pulled up outside Eddie's place with my mascara smeared down my face. I peered in the visor mirror and rubbed under my eyes, trying my best not to appear like I was auditioning for *Panda: The Musical*. If such a show existed.

I touched up my face with my compact, applying some lipstick and fluffing out my bobbed hair. Eddie had always encouraged me to look my best, saying how I could light up a room when I was properly put together, and I wanted him to see me looking good tonight—even if I felt like a piece of crap stuck to the bottom of my shoe.

Try as I might, I couldn't get the look on Nash's face from my mind. He looked . . . wounded, like I'd hurt him deeply. The pangs of guilt returned with a vengeance.

He looked how I felt.

There was a rap on my window, and I almost jumped out of the driver's seat. It was Eddie, peering in at me, concern etched on his face. He opened the door, and I stepped out, up into his embrace. To my embarrassment, fresh tears stung my eyes. I tried to blink them away. I didn't want Eddie to know how upset I truly was.

"Oh, babe," he said, taking me by the shoulders and fixing me with his stare. "You did the right thing."

I nodded. "I know. I feel bad for him, though."

"He's a guy. He'll get over it faster than you know."

He would? I looked at Eddie sharply. Is that what happened with him and me? He got over me fast?

"I hope so."

Eddie wrapped his arm around my shoulders, and we walked the short distance to his apartment building. "He's probably already flicking through his contacts, looking for your replacement."

"Yeah, probably." I knew Eddie was only trying to make me feel better about dumping Nash, but I didn't like hearing it. Did Nash have a replacement in mind already? I thought of him, at his home with Dexter and Gretel and her cute puppies. I imagined Lucky, licking and nuzzling him, as she'd done to me. I swallowed down an uncomfortable feeling in my throat.

"How about we order in and watch a movie together?" Eddie suggested as we waited for the elevator.

"That sounds great."

Once on the fifth floor, Eddie slotted his key in his apartment door. Swinging it open, I walked over the threshold and peered around. He had a stunning view of the city and out toward the harbor, and his place looked just like the New York lofts you saw in the movies.

"Wow, Eddie, this place is great." I dropped my purse on the table and walked around, taking in the high ceiling, the industrial lighting, the plain white walls, the dark hardwood floors. It looked like he'd taken an image of a New York loft to an interior decorator and said, "Give me this." There was even an oversized black-and-white picture of the Manhattan skyline hanging over the sofa to complete the look.

"Thanks, babe. I'm glad you approve. I had a place like this in New York, so when I moved back, I decided to replicate it here." He pulled me in to him and kissed me on the lips. It felt nice, reassuring, familiar —which, of course, it was. "Drink?" he offered, letting go of me and heading toward the open plan kitchen. "Let me guess, you're still on a diet so you'd like a vodka, lime, and soda."

I smiled, remembering how I had researched the lowest calorie alcohol when I had made the decision to lose weight. Vodka, lime, and soda water was right down there in the calorie stakes, and it was always my drink of choice back then. "Sure, that would be nice." I took a seat on one of the plush sofas. "When did you move back?"

"Oh, about two years ago," he replied, his head in the refrigerator.

Two years? That was a long time for him to have been back in Auckland and not try to see me. I shrugged it off. He was involved with someone else. The last thing he would have been thinking about was starting something up with me again.

But then he did say no one ever compared with me.

"Look, I don't have any limes, so is vodka and soda water okay?"

It sounded completely disgusting and tasteless, but I nodded and smiled, wanting the evening to go as perfectly as our day on the beach had. If that meant drinking a frankly weird drink, then bring it on.

We sat on the sofa—me with my vodka and soda water with no ice (he didn't have any of that, either), and Eddie with a glass of red wine, his chosen tipple, even back in college. We clinked glasses.

"Here's to us."

I took a sip. Yup, just as bad as it sounded. I smiled at Eddie and he returned it tenfold.

"I'm so happy you're mine."

I smiled at the memory. He always used to say, "you're mine" back when we were together. It was one of his things. It had made me feel wanted, needed, part of an inseparable couple.

Until we weren't.

"Me too," I said, leaning in for another kiss. "Tell me again how you knew I was The One?" I knew I was being childish, but I didn't care. Hearing this story from Eddie validated my choice to hold out for him all these years—and to be with him and not Nash.

He smiled indulgently at me. "When I saw you at that café, laughing with your friends, looking more beautiful than ever, I just knew."

I beamed at him. Eddie just knew, the way people said you did when you found The One.

"Now can we order in and watch that movie?"

I nodded and snuggled back into him, enjoying our closeness. I had made my choice and it was Eddie. Nice, reassuring, familiar, Eddie.

* * *

THE FOLLOWING MORNING, back from my morning run, showered and dressed, ready for work, I was busy in the kitchen preparing my breakfast and a cup of coffee. I was practicing singing "Thinking Out Loud," ready for my upcoming performance, when Ryan shuffled in.

"Morning!" I trilled. It was a beautiful, sunny day, things were going well at work, and I had Eddie back. Everything had fallen into place, just the way I had hoped it would when I had decided to go on my those Last First Dates, all those weeks ago.

"You're in a good mood." He pulled out a barstool and slumped down onto it, resting his hands heavily on the counter with a sigh.

He, clearly, was not.

"I am." I grinned at him. "Coffee?"

"Yeah, thanks. I could do with mainlining it today."

"Rough night?" I inquired as I poured him a cup.

"Nothing out of the ordinary, I guess. I can't seem to summon the energy to get up in the morning, even though I sleep like the dead."

"That, my dear brother, is called depression. You need to kick that in the butt, starting by coming out on my morning run with me. Six a.m. tomorrow."

He groaned his response. "We're not all in love with Nash, you know."

A sudden coldness hit me in the core at the mention of Nash's name. "No, I . . ." I knew I had to start telling people about me and Eddie, and Ryan was as good a place to start as any. "I've, ah, been seeing Eddie, actually." I passed Ryan a mug of coffee, leaned back against the counter, and waited tentatively for his response.

"Who's Eddie?" Ryan asked, looking confused, picking up his mug.

"You know. Eddie Sutcliffe?"

"Your ex-boyfriend, Eddie?"

I nodded, unable to suppress the grin spreading across my face.

Ryan scrunched up his face. "The Eddie who tore your heart out and trampled on it? *That* Eddie?"

I shifted my weight from foot to foot. To be fair, he had done that. And it had taken me a long time to recover. But that was in the past. The important thing was he was back, and he wanted to be with me.

I let out a sigh. I knew I would have to explain the sudden redirection of my affections from Nash to Eddie, and I had a speech prepared and ready to go. "Eddie was young back then, Ryan, and he didn't know what he wanted. Now, he knows he wants me. When he came back into my life, I realized I still loved him and it wouldn't be fair to remain with Nash, knowing how I felt."

Ryan scratched his head, mussing up his already ruffled sandy blond hair. "When the heck did that happen? You were out with Nash and the rest of us only a few nights ago."

I shrugged. "Saturday."

He shook his head. "You work fast."

"Well, when you know, you know."

Ryan took a sip of his coffee. "Yeah, I thought I knew with Amelia," he replied glumly.

I refused to let my miserable brother get me down, today of all days. And anyway, hadn't he been flirting with half the women at the Cozy Cottage Café on Friday night?

"Okay. I get it. You're still hung up on Amelia. I've been there, believe me."

"Eddie?" he asked.

"Oh, yes, Eddie. He said he had been subconsciously comparing every woman he dated with me, and that's exactly what I had been doing, too."

"What are you saying? I should hang out for Amelia to change her mind and come back to me?"

I nodded. "Maybe."

"How long did it take with Eddie? Ten years? That's too long for me to wait. I'm already in my thirties." His shoulders slumped once more.

"It was only seven years, but that's not the point."

"*Only* seven years?" he replied, his eyes wide. "You're a special kind of crazy, you know that, sis?"

"Look, my point is, you've got to follow your heart. I did and look where I am now. I've got Eddie back." I smiled, thinking about our weekend together, how he had told me he could never imagine loving another woman as he loved me. "Ryan, if your heart tells you Amelia's The One, you can't give up hope."

He picked his coffee mug up and took a sip. I did the same, waiting for his response.

"I guess," was all he offered. With another heavy sigh, he pushed himself up from the stool and shuffled toward the hall. He turned and smiled at me. "I'm glad you got what you wanted."

I returned his smile, my heart contracting at the thought of wonderful Eddie. "Me too."

* * *

LATER THAT MORNING, I sat at our regular table in the window of the Cozy Cottage, mentally preparing myself to tell my friends about Eddie. Even though they had universally given Nash the thumbs-up, I hoped they wouldn't particularly care who I was with, as long as I had chosen *someone* as my Last First Date. Eddie was as good as any of them—better, even. He'd had my heart for all these years, after all. Who better than my first love to be my last? And he was a "good catch," as they used to say: a high-flying corporate lawyer in a top firm, on the partner track, with a great apartment, and still as cute as he always was.

Sophie, dressed in her Cozy Cottage Café apron over a T-shirt and a pair of jeans, delivered my cup of coffee and slice of orange and almond syrup cake with her habitual smile. "Are you on your own today?"

"No, I'm meeting Cassie, and I had hoped Bailey and Paige could join me, but"—I looked over at the empty counter—"I haven't seen them."

"Oh, they're out back, plotting and planning something. You know how they are."

"I do." I smiled, thinking how enthusiastic those two were about the Cozy Cottage. They had found their meaning, their "why," their passion in life.

Like Nash.

A sucker punch hit me in the belly. *No. I can't think of him.*

I cleared my throat. "Okay. Do you think you could ask them both to come out for a moment when Cassie gets here? I need to tell them something."

"I'm here," Cassie said, dropping her purse on the table and pulling out a chair. "And that sounds juicy."

I smiled at her in what I hoped was an enigmatic way.

"Sure, I'll go ask them. Do you want a coffee, Cassie?" Sophie asked.

"Oh, yes. And a slice of my usual, too."

"Got it."

With Sophie gone, Cassie asked. "So? What's happened? I bet it's something to do with Nash."

I pressed my lips together, my stomach churning. "Let's wait until the others are here, okay?"

"I guess. But you could give me a hint, right?"

I shook my head. I wanted to do this once and once only. Not counting Ryan, of course. Or Nash. Okay, so I wanted only to have to do this *one* more time.

Not a moment too soon, Paige and Bailey arrived at the table. Neither of them were wearing their Cozy Cottage aprons, and they looked odd to me in their regular clothes. They pulled up chairs and sat down.

"What's the big news?" Bailey asked.

"Can we guess? Because I've got a pretty good idea," Paige said.

"What do think it is?" Cassie asked. "My theory is Nash has—"

"Stop!" I yelled, my hands appropriately held up in the "stop sign" position as my stomach churned, like it was making ice cream. The last thing I wanted was for my friends to start hypothesizing about what Nash had or had not done. We needed to all move on from him and focus on my future with the man of my dreams.

All eyes trained on me, I took a deep breath, preparing to deliver the speech I had given Ryan only a few short hours before. I clenched my fists, trying to release some of my tension. It didn't work.

Why was this proving to be so difficult for me?

"Okay. So, you know how I took the pact with you guys to find The One?"

They all nodded, watching me closely.

"Well, I've found him." My face creased into a smile.

"We know!" Cassie replied at the same time as Paige exclaimed, "We're so happy for you!" and Bailey said, "Nash is so great."

I clenched my hands once more. "It's not . . . him."

My three friends' faces dropped.

"Wait . . . what?" Paige said, her face scrunched up in obvious confusion.

I swallowed. "It's Eddie. I bumped into him on Friday. Here, actually."

"But you were on a date with Nash on Friday night," Bailey said, shaking her head, confusion written on her face.

"Oh!" Paige exclaimed, and all eyes swiveled in her direction. "That was the guy you were talking to, the one with your jacket."

I nodded, an image of a nervous Eddie, holding my jacket in his hands, popped into my mind. "That's him."

"Hold on, let's back up the bus here for a second, shall we?" Cassie said. "You're saying you met a guy while you were on a date with Nash, and now you've decided *he's* The One?"

"It's not like that. Eddie's my ex."

Paige's brows shot up into her hair. "Your ex?"

I nodded. "Yes, we broke up seven years ago. Eddie was young and didn't know what he wanted. Now, he knows he wants me. When he came back into my life, I realized I still loved him and it wouldn't be fair to remain with Nash, knowing how I felt."

My speech delivered, almost word for word with the one I had given Ryan, I sat back in my seat, letting out a heavy sigh.

And then the questions rolled in.

"But what about Nash?"

"How did it happen?"

"Are you in love with him?"

"How do you know he's the right one for you?"

"Have you told Nash?"

I glanced out the window as a man in a dark navy suit walked past, making my belly flip-flop. He smiled and waved at me as he walked toward the café door.

He was right on time.

"I can answer all of your questions, but I have someone I want you all to meet first."

Cassie's forehead crinkled. "You do?"

I stood up, my chair scraping across the hardwood floor. I watched, my heart expanding, as Eddie took a few short steps across the café and was by my side, wrapping his arm around my waist and pulling me in for a quick kiss. I mouthed "hello" to him and turned to face my friends, a wide grin on my face. All three of them were regarding us with slackened jaws, clearly trying to comprehend the recent change in events.

"Everyone, this is Eddie. Eddie, these are my best friends."

I introduced everyone, my friends being their usual polite selves, despite darting one another confused looks.

We had an unwritten rule in our group: you didn't bring a guy to the Cozy Cottage unless you were serious about him. It had always been our place, a girls' space, where we could chat and solve the world's problems over a slice or two of cake. Having Eddie meet us here sent a clear message: he's The One for me.

"Shall I pull up a seat?" Eddie asked.

"Oh, here. Have mine," Paige replied, standing up. "I need to go help Sophie anyway. It was, err, nice to meet you, Eddie." With a quick glance at Cassie and Bailey, Paige retreated to the counter.

Eddie sat down next to me, placing his hand in mine. It was warm and reassuring, just what I needed right now. I shot him a grateful look.

"So, ah, Eddie, is it?" Cassie asked.

He smiled and nodded. "That's right, Eddie Sutcliffe."

"Tell us a little about yourself."

"Marissa said you might do this. Okay, my full name is Edward Simon Sutcliffe, I work as a corporate lawyer at Preston, Meyers, and Brown, and I'm recently returned to Auckland after a few years in The Big Apple—that's New York, in case you didn't know."

"I think we both got that, right, Bailey?" Cassie said, shooting Bailey a look.

She nodded. "We did."

"And, I imagine you want to know how this all happened with Marissa."

My friends nodded.

He turned to look at me. "I guess I was asleep, and when I saw her, I woke up." His face broke into a smile.

I smiled back at him, wondering what my friends thought. Was it just me or was that a little cheesy?

"So, now that you're 'awake,' as you put it," Cassie said, her fingers doing air quotes as she bit back a smile, "are you serious about Marissa?"

"I get it. You're worried I'm going to swoop in and break her heart again."

"I don't think we knew you'd broken Marissa's heart in the first place," Bailey commented, her brows shooting up into her hairline. "Did we?" She looked from Cassie to me.

Beneath the table, I crossed and uncrossed my legs. I had never told my friends about Eddie and what he'd done. It had happened so long ago, I figured it wasn't relevant. I mean, who likes to talk about their heart being broken? Well, other than Ryan, who didn't seem to be able to talk about much else these days.

"We . . . we dated a long time ago," I said.

Eddie squeezed my hand, and I shot him another grateful look. "And I made the biggest mistake of my life, letting this one go."

"Well, you didn't 'let me go,' exactly," I replied, regretting it instantly.

"No, I didn't. I was a fool." He looked from me to my friends. "But I'm here to stay now. I'm hers, and she's mine." He turned back to me. "If you'll have me."

My heart beat hard in my chest. "Of course."

An awkward silence followed, in which Eddie and I smiled at my friends, awaiting their verdict. Finally, Bailey said, "Well, I think it's wonderful you've found one another again."

I watched closely as she looked at Cassie, prompting her to speak. "Yes, absolutely," she said, nodding her head with vigor.

I let out a relieved breath. I knew they were both putting on a front and being positive about this man they only just met a matter of minutes ago. They needed time to get used to the idea of him and me. They had only just met Nash, after all. I was certain they would grow to like Eddie the more they got to know him.

"Now, Eddie. Would you like a cup of coffee?" Bailey asked, standing up.

"Sure, but I'll go get it. There's a barista over there." He looked around the café. "This is a . . . how would you describe it? A 'quaint' place, I guess."

I cleared my throat. "Bailey owns this café."

"Really? Good for you," Eddie said, smiling up at her.

"Thanks." I felt a twist of discomfort as I noticed Bailey's perpetual smile drop a fraction.

"I would like a black coffee, please. No sugar, extra strong."

"Coming right up. Cassie, I'll leave the lovebirds to you." Bailey returned to the counter, and Eddie and I were left at the table with Cassie.

"Gosh, in all the excitement, I totally forgot to eat my cake!" she exclaimed, picking up her fork.

"Bailey and Paige make the best cakes," I explained to Eddie. "And we all have our favorites. Cassie's is the flourless chocolate and rasp-berry cake, Paige's is the carrot cake with cream cheese frosting, and mine is orange and almond syrup cake. See?" I pushed the plate with the slice of cake on it toward Eddie. "I'm not sure what Bailey's

151

favorite is. Do you know, Cassie?" I picked up my fork and sunk it into the moist cake.

Her mouth full of chocolate cake, Cassie shook her head. "Uh-ah."

"I must ask her." I slipped the cake into my mouth and immediately cut off another piece. "Mm, so good. Here." I offered my fork to Eddie who took it from me and slipped it into his mouth.

"Wow, yes. That is delicious."

"Right?" I grinned at him, happy I could share my love of Cozy Cottage cakes with him.

"I can see one change in you," Eddie said with a smile.

"What's that?" I took another mouthful of cake.

"You're not as concerned with watching your weight as you once were."

The cake in my mouth turned to sawdust. I stole a glance at Cassie. Her eyebrows were raised, and she was looking at Eddie, blinking.

With effort, I swallowed my mouthful and smiled. "Eddie knew me when I was always dieting, you see. I've never told you this, but . . . I had a bit of a weight problem when I was a teenager."

"Oh, I see." Cassie nodded at me. "Well, you don't now. She looks amazing, don't you think?" she asked Eddie.

"Oh, yes. Beautiful."

I beamed at him. Okay, so he may have made the kind of comment no woman wanted to hear, but he had made up for it. Plus, in his defense, I was always dieting back then, before I knew how important exercise and eating a balanced diet was.

I slid my fork into the cake once more to take another bite. As I raised it to my mouth, I felt Eddie's hand on mine. I looked over at him in surprise. He shook his head, almost imperceptibly. I returned the fork to the plate.

He was right. What was his saying back then? "A moment on the lips, a lifetime on the hips." Yeah, I remembered that. Not that I'd had a weight issue for many years. I may not be a supermodel, but I was slim enough, and I enjoyed my food. I could forgo the cake, if it brought up some negative feelings for Eddie. It was no big deal.

I smiled again at Cassie, who looked down and started shoveling her cake into her mouth as though this were her last meal on planet Earth.

"Here you go. One coffee, on the house." Bailey placed a cup of black coffee on the table in front of Eddie.

"Thank you so much, that's kind of you," he said, shooting her his dazzling smile.

If Eddie were to have a Hollywood doppelgänger, it would have to be James Marsden, for his smile alone.

Huh. I had never given Eddie a movie star look-alike. I wondered why.

He picked up his coffee cup and took a sip. "That hits the spot. Now, Cassie, tell me about yourself. How do you know Marissa?"

"We work together," she replied, dabbing her face with a napkin, her chocolate and raspberry cake devoured.

"Cassie's my boss, the best I've ever had," I explained.

"Thanks," she replied, collecting her purse. "Look, I've got to run. I've got that . . . appointment. Eddie, it was great to meet you." She smiled at him, stood up, and offered him her hand.

"You, too," he replied, standing up as the gentleman I remembered him to be.

"See you back in the office," Cassie said to me as she beat a hasty retreat.

Eddie and I sat back down, and he slipped his hand into mine once more. "That went well," he commented. "They seem really nice."

"Yes, yes, they are." I bit my lip. I knew Cassie, and despite what Eddie thought, that did not go well.

Well, that's just too bad for her. She would have to suck it up. Eddie was here to stay, and I was completely ecstatic about it.

CHAPTER 17

hen I got back to work after my coffee date with Eddie, I saw a note on my desk. It was from Cassie, asking me to come to her office as soon as I could.

I slipped my purse strap off and walked across the sales floor toward Cassie's office. I noticed a number of people were watching me, so I smiled at them as I strode by.

I knew exactly what Cassie was going to say. She would tell me she didn't like the way Eddie had told me not to eat cake and that she preferred Nash over him.

I locked my jaw, ready for the onslaught.

"I know what you're going to say," I began as I walked into her office.

"I don't think you do." She got up from behind her desk and walked over to me, closing the door. "Take a seat."

I sat down on one of her leather chairs and crossed my legs. "Eddie's a great guy. Please, give him a chance."

"This isn't about Eddie, although I can't say I exactly warmed to him."

Tell me something I didn't already know. "What's it about then?"

She let out a puff of air. "Antoinette."

I nodded, awaiting further information.

"She's laid a formal complaint against you."

"What?!" I levitated off my seat. A formal complaint? This was insanity! "When? Why?"

"Try and calm down, okay?" Cassie said.

"Calm down? Antoinette of the Amish has laid a formal complaint against me and you want me to *calm down*?"

"I know. It's crazy, but it's true. I just got off the phone with Laura Carmichael," Cassie said, naming Antoinette's aunt, the reason why Antoinette got the job at AGD in the first place. "Laura said Antoinette came to her with it. She totally bypassed me."

I sat back in my seat and crossed my arms. I racked my brain for any clue as to what Antoinette could possibly have to complain about me. I came up with nothing. Tapping my foot on the floor, I said, "Tell me what it's about."

Cassie let out a puff of air. "She's accused you of bullying in the workplace."

My jaw dropped open as I gawped at her. "I haven't bullied her!"

"She said you told her she dressed and acted unprofessionally in the office and said she would fail as an Account Manager if she didn't change."

"What? No, I didn't." My mind began to race. "Although, she did start to wear those sack dresses like she was in a Laura Ingalls Wilder novel after she asked me whether she dressed appropriately for the office." I let out a bitter laugh. "Well, except for a bonnet."

Cassie sucked in air. "What exactly did you say to her?"

"I don't remember my precise words. All I said was that she might like to dial back on the obvious sex appeal a little."

Cassie pulled a face and shook her head. "That's not good, Marissa."

"Oh, come on!" I leaped out of my chair. "She looked like she was an extra on the set of *Baywatch*, for goodness' sakes. You saw her! It was hardly professional with the big hair and the boobs on display." I gestured at my own modest chest.

"I did, but I didn't say anything to her."

155

I began to pace the room. "Look, I only mentioned it because she asked for my help."

How could Antoinette do this to me? I had taken her under my wing, shown her how to do her job, given her useful advice on a whole host of things—advice I would have liked when I first started out.

"Antoinette was the one who decided to take it to the limit. I never suggested she dress like *that*."

"I get it, and I'm talking to you as your friend here. But, there's something else."

I slumped down in my chair. "What is it?"

"She said you told her not to 'sexualize' herself in the office."

"Come again?"

"It's the term her lawyer's used."

My eyes nearly popped out of my head. "Her *lawyer?*" I buried my head in my hands. "Oh, no."

"Try to remember what you said to her," Cassie said gently.

I looked up at her from my bent-over position. I let out a heavy sigh. "I don't know. Something about not trying to get everyone's attention."

Cassie's hand darted to her face. She covered her mouth and shook her head. "Oh, no."

"I'm a straight shooter, you know what I'm like." I chewed the inside of my lip. "What's going to happen to me?" To my utter mortification, tears stung my eyes. I never cried at work.

I was one of those consummate professionals: I was there to do a job and do it well. Emotions didn't come into it. But right then, I felt like running to the ladies' for a decent sob fest.

Cassie shook her head again. "I don't know. Laura has asked me to meet with her later. I'll know more then, even though Antoinette could have come to me with this and we could have sorted it out between ourselves without having to involve the exec team. I am her boss, after all."

I narrowed my eyes. "Why do you think she went one step up the organization, to Laura?" My mind whirring, I narrowed my eyes. "What's she playing at?" I drummed my fingers against my chin.

"I don't know. She probably only went to Laura with this because she's her aunt."

"Maybe." Something didn't fit. If she were genuinely upset with what I had said to her, wouldn't she have talked to her boss about it? "Where is Antoinette, anyway? I haven't seen her in the office."

"She's . . . err . . ."

"Why don't you want to tell me?"

"She's taken stress leave."

I let out a sardonic laugh. "Stress leave? Are you serious?" I blinked, running my hands through my hair. All I could hear was the sound of my own breathing as the room began to tilt.

"Marissa!" The next thing I knew, Cassie was crouching down next to me, her hand on my back. "You've gone all pale. Put your head between your knees and breathe."

As if on automatic pilot, I did as instructed. After a few breaths, I began to regain my composure. Embarrassed, I smiled weakly at Cassie. "Thanks. Sorry about that. I don't know what came over me."

"You had a shock. Take a moment."

"Nothing like this has ever happened to me before." I had always been professional at work, always giving it my all. I took my job seriously, and I enjoyed it. I looked at Cassie. "What should I do?"

"I suggest you lay low, get on with your job, and wait. Once I've seen Laura, I'll have a clearer idea of what we're dealing with here."

"And what Antoinette really wants."

"Maybe? It's still too unclear."

I nodded, swallowing back those pesky tears. "Thanks."

"Hey, I've got your back one hundred percent."

I smiled weakly at her. For a moment there, I thought I had it all. Now, with my career hanging in the balance, I needed my friends—and Eddie—more than ever.

* * *

I BUMBLED through the rest of the work day, trying hard not to let Antoinette's complaint get to me. There was a process for these sorts of things, and Cassie would help me as much as she could. I would pull through it, and everyone would be able to see Antoinette was an attention-seeking piece of work who took a well-intentioned comment out of context.

Sitting across from Eddie at the Thai Elephant, my favorite local Thai restaurant, I let out a heavy sigh. "I don't get why she's doing this to me."

"It's because she sees you as a threat," he replied matter-of-factly.

"Why?"

"She's being an alpha female. She's marking her territory, and you are in her way."

I pictured Antoinette urinating in spots around the office, marking out her territory. I would have laughed if I hadn't been so depressed. "Is alpha female a thing?" I thought back to high school science. I didn't recall any reference to alpha females, although there were definitely a whole lot of alpha males, causing loads of trouble.

"Diva, then. Let's call her a diva. She wants to get rid of you so she can rule the roost."

Unconvinced, I mumbled, "I guess."

"Trust me. I know about these things."

The waiter delivered our meals. Eddie had ordered my favorite green chicken curry, whereas, after the whole cake thing this morning, I had gone for a small prawn salad. Eddie's smelled amazing, and I ended up wolfing my meal down in record time, still hungry for more.

At the end of the meal, Eddie paid and we walked the short distance through the city streets to my apartment, arm in arm. It felt so good to be back together with him, and it was proving to be everything I had ever dreamed it would be.

"Hey, I'm going to a swap meet on Saturday. I'm hoping you'll come with me," Eddie said.

"What sort of swap meet?"

"Motorcycle, of course," he replied as though there could be no other sort and I had, quite possibly, lost my mind.

I smiled at him, shaking my head. Eddie had always loved motor-cycles, and I had to say, it was one of the things I had first noticed about him. He would turn up at campus on his bike, looking super hot and sexy in his beaten up, old brown leather jacket and black helmet. He would slink off his bike, looking all studly and cool, and then, he'd slip his helmet off and ruffle his dark hair with his fingers. It never failed to make me sigh. In fact, half my class were in deep lust with him, and I suspected it was mainly due to his bike. There was simply something about a hot guy on a motorbike I found hard to resist.

"Of course. Yes, I'd love to go to a motorcycle swap meet with you."

Although going to a swap meet with a bunch of motorcycle enthu-siasts had limited appeal, bikes were a part of who Eddie was. He was passionate about them, so I needed to at least show an interest. It was a small price to pay to be with the man of my dreams.

My mind betrayed me, darting to Nash and his passion for dogs. I blinked thoughts of him away. I was with Eddie now. I needed to forget Nash.

Eddie smiled back at me. "Great. It'll be just like old times."

I threw my head back and laughed. "As long as I don't have to sit on the side of the road while you tinker with your bike like I did back then." I had spent many a weekend, dressed up to go out to some party or dinner, waiting for Eddie to finish doing whatever it was he was doing to his bike. I can't say it was my favorite memory of our time together.

"I thought you loved that," he replied, looking wounded. "It was special you and me time, wasn't it?"

"Of course, it was. I was only kidding," I replied hastily, not wanting him to think otherwise. So what if I didn't have fond memo-ries of being late for parties because I had spent two hours waiting for him to work on his bike? It was no big deal then, and it would be no big deal now. "It will be like old times. Just like old times."

He stopped and looked at me. His eyes sparkled. "I love you, Marissa."

My belly did a flip as my heart rate picked up. "You love me?" I asked, breathless, barely believing his words.

"Yes, silly. What did you think?" He touched his fingers to my cheek. "We're back together and this is it for me. *You* are it for me. I want to be your forever."

I could have exploded with happiness. I hurled myself at him, collecting him in a hug and peppering him with kisses. "Oh, Eddie! I love you, too. I always, always have."

And I knew it was the truth. Even when Eddie had left me, leaving my heart in tatters, I had never stopped loving him. And now he was back, it was going to work—it *had* to work.

If he wanted me to be his forever, I wanted him to be mine.

Only, I didn't feel quite as happy, quite as euphoric, as I thought I would on hearing him say those three little words. This was what I had wanted for so long: perhaps finally getting it, making it real, somehow diminished it?

You're being ridiculous, Marissa.

I pushed any doubts I had from my mind. I needed to concentrate on being with Eddie, the man I loved.

Second-guessing anything would do nothing but cause trouble.

CHAPTER 18

*A*t work the following day, I took the flight of stairs up to meet with Laura Carmichael, as nervous as a bride on her wedding day. Only this wasn't a good nerves situation. Oh, no. Quite the opposite. I was on my way to meet with my boss's boss, Human Resources, and that conniving backstabber, Antoinette, to learn my fate. Whoever Antoinette's lawyer was hadn't seen fit to attend. That at least was a small mercy. Not that it made me feel a whole lot better about it all.

Cassie hadn't been able to tell me anything more about the complaint, and I hadn't seen Antoinette in the office since Cassie dropped the bombshell about what she had done.

I was going in blind, and I hated that feeling.

I pushed the door open at the top of the staircase and spotted Cassie, chatting to Brian the Rottweiler, Laura's officious executive assistant. When the door closed with a *thunk* behind me, she looked up and shot me a supportive smile.

"Morning, Cassie, morning, Brian," I said, plastering a smile on my face as though I wasn't about to take the corporate death march.

"Yes, hello," Brian replied, looking me up and down, his eyebrows raised as if to ask, "who threw up on you today?" Answer: Antoinette Smith.

Self-consciously, I glanced down at my usual blouse and pencil skirt combination. Oops! My face flushing, I tucked my blouse in properly and straightened my skirt. I didn't look my usual, polished self today, that was for certain. Not surprising, considering I'd barely slept a wink, worrying about my fate.

Cassie gestured toward the sofas a few feet away from Brian's desk, and I followed her over.

"How are you feeling?" she asked me in a hushed tone.

I shrugged. "Totally stressed out." There was no use beating around the bush.

"I bet. Don't worry, I'll be here with you to support you."

I shot her a grateful smile. "Thanks."

We sat in silence for a few moments, waiting for Rottweiler Brian to call us. I crossed my arms and drummed my fingers on my elbows. This was not fun.

"How are things with Eddie?" Cassie asked in an obvious attempt to distract me from my potential career catastrophe.

My face creased into a smile. "Good. Really good."

"I'm so happy for you. Even though I was Team Nash, of course. The most important thing to me is you're happy."

"I am, and thanks." I pushed Nash's hurt face from my mind. I couldn't cope with thinking about that right now.

"Ladies?" Brian called, bringing me back to the room.

"You ready for this?" Cassie asked as she stood up and smoothed down her skirt.

"I'm going to have to be, aren't I?"

Like a lamb to the slaughter, I stood up and followed Cassie past Brian and into Laura's office. Laura was standing in front of her desk, her arms crossed, watching us. She raised her eyebrows when she spotted me, and I shot her a weak smile. It wasn't returned. *Great.* I glanced at the seating area to my left where Hugo, the usually friendly guy from Human Resources was standing. Next to him was Antoinette, dressed once again like a Vegas hooker slash drag queen, her platinum extensions falling in soft waves to her elbows. I tightened my jaw, and she shot me a self-satisfied smirk.

"Please, take a seat," Laura said.

We all sat down on the plush leather sofas: me next to Cassie, Antoinette next to Laura, and Hugo in the middle. I swallowed. The battle lines had been drawn.

"May I begin?" Hugo said, looking at Laura. She nodded, and he continued, "Thank you all for being here." I narrowed my eyes across the coffee table to Antoinette. *Like I had a choice.* "As you are all aware, Antoinette Smith has laid a formal complaint against Marissa Jones on the basis Marissa put unreasonable pressure on her to look and behave in a way Antoinette was not comfortable with."

"It limited my self-expression," Antoinette added, her chin held high.

"Right, yes. Your, ah . . . your self-expression," Hugo repeated.

"And it damaged my self-esteem," Antoinette added, dabbing her eyes with a tissue for dramatic effect.

Although I was sorely tempted to refute the claim, knowing her self-esteem was fully intact, I bit my tongue. Instead, I rolled my eyes so hard, they could have fallen out of my head. Where did this woman get off?

"Yes, absolutely, your self-esteem," Hugo said, nodding at Antoinette. "So, we're here to try to resolve this allegation and find a way forward."

"That's right, Hugo. Thank you for that introduction," Laura chimed in. She looked directly at me. "Marissa, are you fully aware of the complaint that's been laid against you?"

I glanced at Cassie. Unless she hadn't given me the full picture, the answer was yes.

"She is," Cassie replied on my behalf.

"Good." Laura nodded. "Of course, we want to give you a chance to respond to what Antoinette has said, so please, feel free to have your say."

I looked from Laura to Antoinette. She was still dabbing at her eyes in an Oscar-worthy performance Meryl Streep herself would be proud of.

"Okay, here's what happened." I told them how Antoinette had approached me, asking how she could fit into the team better and whether there was anything I would change about her to help her do so. "So, you see, all I was trying to do was help her in her new job at AGD. I wasn't trying to bully her or anything." I turned to face Antoinette, and even though I would quite like to have taken the box of tissues she had been steadily working through and stuff it down her throat, I smiled at her. "Antoinette, please accept my apology if I said anything that offended you. That was the last thing I wanted to do, and please know all I was trying to do was help."

Which was the truth. I had never intended any of this and had thought Antoinette was genuine in her interest in fitting in at AGD.

More fool me.

Antoinette let out a sob, raising her hand to her forehead as though she could faint like some nineteenth-century heroine. Under different circumstances, I might have found her performance funny. But, the circumstances weren't different, and I definitely did not.

Laura put a comforting hand on Antoinette's back. "Marissa, I think you can learn a valuable lesson here: not to make bold statements about something that is none of your business. Particularly about another person's appearance. Look at her, this has been so hard on poor Antoinette."

My mouth dropped open as "poor Antoinette" rested her head on Laura's shoulder, like she was a wounded five-year-old child in need of comfort.

"Really, Laura, I think Marissa's intentions were commendable," Cassie said, leaping to my defense. "This feels like a situation that has got out of hand, and with a little negotiation, we could put it to bed right now, don't you think?"

Hugo nodded at Cassie, then looked at Laura for her reaction. She pursed her lips. "Look, Marissa, you may as well know Antoinette is my niece."

"Really?" I said, placing my hand on my chest as though this were a big surprise to me.

Laura nodded. "I'm a little more protective over her than perhaps I should be."

"Well, that's entirely understandable, but it doesn't mean we can't resolve this now," Cassie said. She shot me a look.

"Maybe we should see how Antoinette would like to proceed?" Hugo asked.

All eyes turned to Antoinette, who had managed to dribble mascara down her aunt's cream blouse. She sat up straight and dabbed her eyes once more, asking us all, "for a moment." We waited—some of us more patiently than others.

Eventually, she cleared her throat and began, "Maybe Marissa has something she could do f-for me? That would help a lot."

I narrowed my eyes at her. "What would that be?"

"I don't know. Let me think." She tapped her chin, her eyes raised to the ceiling, doing her best Shirley Temple impersonation—if Shirley Temple had hooker hair extensions and breasts the size of melons, that was.

Call me cynical, but it felt utterly staged. This woman knew what she wanted—and how to go about getting it.

"If it's all right with you, Aunty Lore," she began, and Cassie and I shared another look, "I could always have one of the accounts I've been working so hard on with Marissa? I think that would help me."

One of the accounts? Which one? The cogs in my brain began to whirr.

"That may be a good solution. Unorthodox, but if it's what you want to do?" Laura asked her.

Antoinette nodded.

Laura turned to me. "What do you think, Marissa?"

"Which account?" I asked as pleasantly as I could, fearing—*knowing* —her reply.

"I don't know," Antoinette said with a shrug. "Let me think." More chin tapping. "Off the top of my head, how about . . . Pukeko Chocolates?"

My eyes bulged out of my head. She wanted my biggest customer, the one that would help me achieve my annual target early, the one I was relying on to get me the big promotion. "You want Pukeko's?" I squeaked, my eyes darting to Cassie.

"Laura, with all due respect, Marissa has worked very hard on this account. Maybe we could think about another way forward? Perhaps another account?"

Antoinette crossed her arms, pouting. Wow, she really was Shirley Temple.

"I want Pukeko Chocolates, or there's no saying what I'll do," Antoinette said as she glared at me, the threat so lightly veiled you could see through it at one hundred paces.

"Cassie?" Laura said, her eyebrows raised in expectation.

Cassie looked from Laura's face to Antoinette's to mine. She let out a puff of air and put her hand on mine. I darted a pleading look at her. "I know this isn't what you want to hear, but it might be the best solution here, Marissa."

My eyes darted from Cassie to Laura, landing on Antoinette's face. She had a small smirk on her face, her eyes screaming, "Gotcha!"

I clenched my jaw shut. I was well and truly stuck between a rock and a conniving bitch.

I had to resist the almost overwhelming temptation to wrap my fingers around her pretty little neck and squeeze.

Well played, Antoinette, well played.

"What's your response, Marissa?" Hugo asked, interrupting my rather satisfying fantasy.

"I . . ." I knew I was beat. It was either this or something a whole lot worse, perhaps even losing my job, a job I loved. I nodded, pressing my lips together. "All right. I accept the terms. Antoinette can have Pukeko's."

Antoinette smiled and batted her eyelids. "Thank you, Marissa. I am certain your generosity in giving me this account will help me heal."

Good Lord, kill me now.

Laura's face broke into a smile. "That's that, then. Hugo, can you

THREE LAST FIRST DATES

please note the complaint as resolved, and we can all get on with our days." She stood up, signaling the end of the meeting.

As I shuffled, defeated, out of Laura's office, Antoinette shot me a triumphant look before turning away to give "Auntie Lore" a hug. I let out a heavy sigh. She'd gotten what she had set out to get, and I'd been the mug who had helped her achieve it.

* * *

My head still trying to make sense of what Antoinette had done, I arrived at the Cozy Cottage where I had asked Eddie to meet me. I needed his support more now than ever, now my hope of a promotion to Account Director was officially as dead as a dodo.

I stood in line to order, my mind bouncing all over the place. Had Antoinette planned this all along? Had she chosen me that day in the team meeting because I was an easy target? Or was it more about winning the new business, to launch her career as an Account Manager at AGD?

"Hi, Marissa!" Bailey said, grinning at me over the cabinets.

I shook myself out of my reverie and shot her a smile. Even though I had lost Pukeko Chocolates, I still had my job. I should be happy about that. "Hi. How are you doing?"

"I'm great. I'm really looking forward to your performance at the open mic Cozy Cottage Jam. Paige has posted all the promotional stuff about it."

Singing. Now that was something I could look forward to—and dread at the same time. "Oh, me too. It will be realizing a dream for me."

Bailey raised her eyebrows.

"I know that sounds dramatic, but I'd never had the confidence to do it before."

"But you do now, and that's what matters." Her face glowed as she shot me her beautiful smile. "Your usual, I assume?"

I opened my mouth to say "yes," then closed it again. Shaking my head, I replied, "Just a coffee, thanks. A skinny latte. Actually, make that a skinny latte and an extra strong black coffee. I'm meeting Eddie."

"Really? Bringing a boy here again, huh?" She laughed.

After paying, I found a table and sat down heavily. Our usual girls' table was occupied as I was here at an odd time and Bailey hadn't reserved it for me, so I had to make do with one of the smaller tables near the door. It didn't feel the same, but then my mood was hardly conducive to me doing a cheer-leading routine right now.

"Hi, babe."

I pulled myself out of my reverie to smile up at Eddie, standing in front of me. "Hi."

He pulled a chair out and sat down next to me. "How did it go?"

"Weirdly. It turns out all she wanted was this big customer. Shooting me down in the process was just collateral damage."

"So, it wasn't personal? This woman isn't out to get you?"

I shook my head. "I don't think so."

Eddie sat back in his seat. "Well, that's a relief."

"Yeah, I guess." I was too stunned by the morning's events to feel anything, although I knew Eddie was right. For now, at least.

"Here you are," Sophie said, placing the cups of coffee on the table in front of us. "A skinny latte and a black coffee."

"Is it extra hot?" Eddie inquired, looking up at Sophie.

"Sure, it is!"

I darted Sophie a questioning look. She winked at me, turned her back, and returned to the counter.

Eddie took a sip of his coffee, replacing the cup in the saucer in disgust. "Luke warm at best." He looked toward the counter. "Who makes the coffee here?"

Not wanting Eddie to create a scene in the café I loved, I searched my brain for a way to distract him. "I have something exciting to tell you," I said, leaning in to him.

"What is it?"

"See that spot over there by the back wall?" I pointed to an area where a group of tables were currently located, near the fireplace. "I'm going to sing there on the twenty-fifth." My chest expanded with anticipation. I could still barely believe it: *Marissa Jones, Live Performer*. I had been practicing and practicing, hoping to conquer my nerves and deliver a great performance.

"Oh, babe, that's fantastic!"

I beamed at him. My boyfriend, Mr. Supportive. "It's an open mic night at the Cozy Cottage Jam, and Bailey and Paige are letting me sing the first song of the night."

"I'm so happy for you. Have you always liked to sing?"

I squished my eyebrows together. How could Eddie not remember how much singing meant to me? Back then, I was always singing along to the radio, in the shower, wherever the mood hit me. "Yes, I have. You know that. But this is a big thing for me. I've never sung in front of an audience before, so I'm kind of nervous about it."

He rubbed my hand. "You'll do great." He pulled his phone out of his pocket. "Was it the twenty-fifth?" he asked, and I nodded. "Let me see. Oh, darn it. I've got a work dinner that night. It's for partners, too."

My smile dropped a fraction. "Can't you get out of it?"

"Not really. In fact, I was kind of hoping you would come with me. It's at The Salon," he said, naming one of the city's swankiest restaurants. "I thought I would introduce you to the partners as *my* partner. You know, make this thing official." He picked up my hand and kissed it, looking up at me with hope in his eyes.

A satisfied, euphoric feeling swept over me. Eddie wanted to announce us to the world.

I beamed at him. "Really?"

He returned my smile, gripping my hand to his chest. "Really. I've told you already, you're mine. And I never want to lose you again."

My heart contracted. This. This was what I wanted. I let out a contented sigh.

He leaned in and kissed me, the world spinning around us. "I'm sure there will be another open mic night. Why don't you talk to your friends about it? It would really mean a lot to me if you were there at the dinner."

I nodded at him, pressing my lips together. Sure, I was disappointed I wouldn't be performing the song I'd been practicing all this time, but Eddie was right, there would be other chances. Being with Eddie was so much more important than me singing some song to a bunch of people who probably didn't even particularly want to hear me do it.

I needed to look at the bigger picture. And Eddie was the leading man.

CHAPTER 19

*A*t work, Antoinette avoided me like the Black Plague, which suited me just fine. She had stolen my big new customer, wrecked my chances of getting a promotion, and made me look like a jealous, spiteful woman.

Really, *I* should be the one avoiding *her*, not the other way around

She had reverted to her former attention-grabbing attire, turning up each day in seemingly shorter and tighter ensembles, with bigger and blonder hair, leaving about as much to the imagination as a stripper at the end of her set.

The office gossip was all about her and me, and I was certain that old sexist adage "cat fight" was being bandied around O'Dowd's over a beer after work by the "He-Men" salesmen from my team. Although I wanted to scream I had been set up and hadn't done anything wrong, I didn't. Instead, I threw myself into my work in the hopes of making up for the lost revenue Pukeko Chocolates' disappearance from my portfolio had created, and meeting my annual targets on time.

That week, Friday could not have come around fast enough. The idea of two solid days without Antoinette lurking nearby was more appealing than an ice-cold soda on a hot and humid afternoon.

Saturday was the day of the motorcycle swap meet, and I was up bright and early with those early birds who catch the worm, ready to spend the day with my wonderful boyfriend. The swap meet was south of the city, and Eddie wanted to get there early so he didn't miss out on the parts he was looking for, so we set out before the city had even opened its eyes, let alone had its first cup of coffee.

I skipped out the door and down the steps to Eddie, straddling his bike, his helmet held under his arm. I was instantly reminded of him on campus, all those years ago, and my heart squeezed at the memory. We greeted each other with a kiss, and he handed me a hot pink helmet with an image of Smurfette on the side.

I looked at it quizzically. "Smurfette? Really?" I'd liked the *Smurfs* just as much as any other kid, but I would never have said my interest would reach adulthood.

"I'm going to get you your own, I promise."

I looked down at the pink helmet in my hands. "This is . . . your ex's?"

Eddie nodded. "Sorry. Let's buy you one at the swap meet today, okay?"

I nodded, wondering what sort of grown woman wanted a pink helmet with a smiling Smurfette emblazoned on the side. I mean, wasn't she the only female in their entire Smurf species? It was all a bit weird.

"Hop on, baby." Eddie slipped his helmet on over his head and revved the bike's engine. I knew next to nothing about motorbikes— which was really quite miraculous, considering how much time I'd spent watching Eddie tinkering with his over the years—but I could tell this bike was an upgrade from the one he had when we were together. It growled, low and strong.

I slipped the helmet over my head, ignoring the whiff of Eddie's ex's favored perfume, slung my leg over the bike, and wrapped my arms around his waist. He pulled away from the curb, and we were off, zooming through the quiet streets, on an adventure together.

Only it was less an adventure and more like the opposite of an adventure: complete and utter boredom. As I waited at yet another stall for Eddie to buy yet another piece of something metal, my mind began to wander. I looked around at the other people at the swap meet. They were nearly all male, with the odd exception, and most of them appeared to be here alone. I spotted a woman about my age, leaning up against a post to one of the stalls, playing on her phone. She must have felt my eyes on her as she looked up, directly at me. I smiled and rolled my eyes to show I was bored, too. She smiled back, shaking her head.

My eyes skimmed the crowd, wondering if there was anyone here I might know—anything to relieve my boredom. I glanced at the back of a man, standing only ten feet away, and did a double take. I took in his dark, messy hair, his broad shoulders, his shorts and work boots. My heart skipped a beat. Nash. I bit my lip, waiting impatiently for him to turn around.

What would I do if it was him? What would I say? Too late, the man turned and looked directly at me. It wasn't Nash. I smiled at him and looked away. It was a good thing. I was off the hook.

So why did my heart sink to the pit of my stomach?

Eddie appeared at my side, holding something metal in one hand and pushing his wallet into the back pocket of his jeans with the other. "They had exactly the part I needed, can you believe it? This bike I'm restoring is totally coming together."

I ignored the feeling in my belly. "That's great," I said, smiling. I loved the way all this bike stuff made Eddie's face light up.

He took my hand in his and kissed me. "You are amazing, you know that?"

"Yeah," I joked, enjoying the flattery. "Why specifically?"

He shrugged, and we turned to walk away from the stall. "I don't know. You get me. You get that this is a part of who I am."

"You're passionate about it."

"Thank you, yes!"

"I totally get it. It's like me with my singing."

"Oh, yeah!"

For a fraction of a second, I beamed at Eddie, my heart expanding in my chest. He got it. He understood me. It made me feel appreciated, loved. It was a very nice feeling, one I wanted to stick around.

But then, he dropped my hand and walked away from me toward a stall. Turning back, he said excitedly, "They've got it! They've actually got it!"

"What?" I asked, confused.

Weren't we talking about what *I* loved to do, what *I* was passionate about?

Without turning back, he entered the stall and struck up a conversation with a tall, bald, bearded guy who couldn't have been more of a bike cliché if he'd tied a bandana around his head. I stood, openmouthed, watching Eddie talk animatedly to this man, a sense of unease, of déjà vu, rising inside me.

I glanced at the girl I'd had that moment of solidarity with a few minutes ago. She was still staring at her phone, stifling a yawn.

And that's when I remembered. I remembered what it was like, what it was *really* like, back then, when I was with Eddie. Sure, we didn't go to many swap meets because he wasn't restoring a bike back then, but I sure did put in my time while he followed his passion. All those hours, sitting, waiting for him to finish at the side of the road.

And it *did* bother me. It bothered me I would miss out on things I wanted to do, it bothered me when we would be late for events because of him. Sure, Eddie was nice to me, telling me how much it meant that I was always there for him, but I was so lacking in confidence, putting his needs before mine felt natural, right.

I took in a sharp breath as it began to fall into place with a sickening *thud*.

Everything in our relationship was about him. I was riding along with him, but I wasn't the main event in his life.

He was.

"I cannot believe this," he said, appearing by my side once more. "I've got nearly everything I need." He pulled me in and kissed me, his eyes sparkling. "I am so glad you're here with me for this."

"Me too," I muttered, my head spinning.

"Let's go and eat. I am going to treat you to the best green smoothie money can buy." Eddie took my hand, and we made our way through the crowds to the drinks cart.

It was all I could manage to put one foot in front of the other, wondering how I had ended up back here, wondering what I had done.

* * *

INSTEAD OF GOING BACK to Eddie's place that evening, I pleaded exhaustion and bid him goodnight with the promise I would meet with him tomorrow.

"Besides, it will give you more time to work on your bike," I said as we stood outside my apartment building, my fingers interlaced behind his neck.

His face lit up. "True. Marissa, I love you so much. You always know what's best for me."

A bunch of bees began to buzz insistently in my belly. *Just not what's best for* me.

I waved Eddie off and trudged upstairs to my apartment. It was late Saturday afternoon and Ryan, the man almost surgically attached to my sofa, was out. It was just me and my thoughts in my empty apartment.

I placed my purse on the little table by the door and shrugged off my jacket. I walked over to the kitchen. I sighed. I looked out the window. After about zero point three seconds, I'd had enough of the silence. I didn't want to be alone with my thoughts. They were saying things I did not want to hear, things that could change everything for me. And I didn't want to have to listen to them.

I wandered back to my purse and pulled out my phone. I sent off a text to Paige, asking what she was up to. No response. Then, I texted Cassie. Also, no response. I let out a heavy sigh. I needed a distraction, stat!

I texted Bailey and nearly had a heart attack when she messaged me back straightaway. We agreed to meet for a drink at six o'clock, and I headed to the shower to freshen up, my spirits lifted immeasurably by the thought of seeing her—and *not* being alone.

A shower, some makeup, and a cute dress thrown on later, I met Bailey at O'Dowd's.

"You look so glamorous," I said, taking in her strappy black dress with the nipped-in waist, showcasing her hourglass figure to perfection.

"Oh, you're just used to seeing me in my apron. Anything says 'glamour' after a 'pinny.'"

I chuckled. Bailey was one of those women who always looked good, no matter what. Really, by the rules of the urban jungle, I should hate her, but I don't. She's simply Bailey, my sweet, thoughtful friend who bakes the best cakes this end of the Pacific Ocean. "I guess. Can I buy you a drink?"

"Yes, that would be wonderful, thanks. I'll have a whiskey sour, please."

I raised my eyebrows. With her Italian looks, I'd expected her to order a *vino rosso* with a side order of mozzarella, not a cocktail that sounded like something my dad would drink. "One whiskey sour coming up."

Bailey and I perched on a couple of stools, side by side. We hadn't spent much time one-on-one together since we had set about finding a man for Paige—a job well done on our part, I might add—and it was nice to get the chance to spend some quality time with her.

Well, it would have been had I not had the emotional turmoil raging inside.

We waited to place our drinks order. I hoped not to get Blaze's friend, Buff, serving me. Although Blaze and I had parted company on good terms, I couldn't handle any potential comments from his friend —not tonight.

Buff finished serving a young, bearded guy, who walked away, balancing an impressive number of beers in his hands, and turned to me. "Hey," he said, doing that chin-raising thing he did when I was here with Blaze.

"Hey," I replied with a smile.

"You know Blaze, right?"

"Yeah. How is he?"

"Good. Awesome. You know Blaze." He shrugged. "He's always on top form, that dude."

"Good, great," I replied, awkward. I quickly placed our drinks order.

"I wouldn't have picked you as a whiskey drinker," I said to Bailey, doing my best to ignore the bees buzzing up a storm in my belly.

Seriously, go find a hive!

"Oh, I'm hardly what you'd call a 'whiskey drinker,' but I am part Irish, you know. I think it's the law to drink it up there."

I chuckled. I didn't know she was part Irish, either. Somehow that made her seem more approachable, less like the exotic Italian screen siren I always thought of her as.

"Oh, before I forget, I need to let you know, I won't be singing at the Jam as I'd originally thought."

"Oh, no! Why not? I thought you were really keen. Has something come up?"

"As a matter of fact, yes. And it's a good thing. You see, Eddie's got a work dinner and he wants me to go to it with him. It's kind of like him announcing us as a serious couple," I said, quoting Eddie.

The bees began an elaborate skydiving routine.

She narrowed her eyes at me. "But—"

"Here you go, ladies. A whiskey sour and a glass of chardonnay," Buff interrupted her, delivering our drinks.

"Thanks," we both said.

"I made yours extra special," he said to Bailey, a flirty smile on his face. He was being about as subtle as a sledgehammer.

"Thanks," she repeated, returning his smile.

"So, ah, let me know when you want another one. Buff's the name, you know, because I'm *buff*." He did that thing bodybuilders like to do: clenching his chest and pulling his arms across his torso, presumably to make himself look more . . . buff?

I was certain I heard a ripping sound and had to stifle a giggle, assuming it was either his T-shirt or his pants—though my money was on his pants.

"I'll do that. Thank you," Bailey said graciously, ignoring the

177

clenched muscles on display for her benefit. She turned to me. "Shall we get a table?"

I pressed my lips together, trying my best not to laugh. "I think that would be for the best."

We picked up our drinks and walked to a table about as far away from the bar as we could manage, and both burst into laughter. It felt good to think about something other than Eddie for a change, those bees a distant hum.

We sat down, and I glanced back over at the bar. "'Buff the buff barman' is still watching you. I think you should wave, maybe blow him a kiss?"

Bailey shook her head, smiling. "That would be mean."

"I guess. But really fun." I took a sip of my chardonnay. "Hey, he could be your Last First Date!"

She laughed. "Ah, no? I'm holding out for someone special." She took a sip of her whiskey sour. "The man may be a little muscle-obsessed, but he makes a mean drink. Now, please explain how you're letting Eddie's work thing get in the way of your singing? I thought you really wanted to do this?"

"I do. It's just . . ." I struggled with trying to work out what to say, or even how I felt about it. When Eddie had asked me to go to his work dinner, the way he'd explained it had totally swayed me. It had made sense. Now, in the light of my swap meet epiphany, if that's what it was, I wasn't so sure. I let out a sigh and shook my head. "I don't know."

Bailey cocked her head and frowned. "Is everything okay?"

"Yes, of course," I replied with conviction—a conviction I was not feeling.

"I'm sorry, Marissa, but that sounds like you're trying to tell yourself you're okay when in fact you're not."

I bit my lip. I had wanted to go out for a fun evening with a friend tonight so I wasn't alone with my thoughts. But, I guess, sometimes you can't run away. I pressed my lips together, Eddie weighing heavily on my mind. Friends talked to one another about their problems. Maybe I should talk to Bailey?

In the end, I caved. Those bees seemed to have taken up permanent residence in my belly. I had to do something. "I don't know. Eddie's great." Was it? "It's just . . ."

"Just what?" Bailey asked gently.

"I guess there are some things that haven't changed about him, things I'd forgotten about."

"Like?"

"Like the way he's obsessed with motorbikes."

"Hold on there," she said, her palms up. "Guys on motorbikes are super-hot, especially good-looking ones like Eddie."

I smiled. Eddie did have a hint of Ewan McGregor about him when he was on his bike, all manly and in control. It was very sexy. "True. But not when you spend all day at a motorcycle swap meet."

"Ah, good point. But relationships, *good* relationships, are give and take. You support him; he supports you."

I chewed the inside of my lip. "That's the thing. I'm not sure he does."

I explained how Eddie didn't seem to understand how much my singing meant, the fact he hadn't even remembered it was something I liked to do. "And he's kind of controlling, too," I added, finally putting that vague, unsettled feeling I'd had since he turned back up into my life into words.

"The cake thing?" she asked.

"Yeah, the cake thing, and other stuff. I know it's because he wants me to look my best, but it kind of bothers me." I let out a heavy sigh, defeated. "I don't know. I thought when we got back together it would be everything I had hoped. Only . . . it's not."

"Honey, can I say something?" I nodded. "I think you've been in love with someone who doesn't really exist."

My mouth dropped open. I wasn't expecting that! "What did you say?" My voice was thin, high.

"Look, this is only my humble opinion, and I hope I'm not stepping over the line here, but it seems to me you've been putting Eddie on a pedestal all this time, and no other guy has stood a chance."

I nodded. It was possible . . . probable, even. I curled my toes in my shoes. Maybe Eddie did love me? And then again, maybe I was the only mug who would put up with his self-absorption, his total lack of understanding of another's needs.

"And now you've realized Eddie's not who you remembered him to be. He's not perfect, he's a flawed human being like the rest of us. And not only that, there are some things you may not have been bothered about before that don't work for you now."

"I . . . I guess," I managed, my head whirring. I picked up my glass of wine and took a slug.

Not for the first time in the last few days, tears stung my eyes. It all came flooding back: the control, the manipulation, the way he made me feel I wasn't good enough, would never be good enough. I knew it was a cliché, but it was like a light had been switched on in my brain and I could see him for who he was for the first time. It was the way he had kept me, downtrodden, under his spell, it was the way he ensured I would never even contemplate looking at another guy.

Because I wasn't good enough.

But now, I wasn't that girl, the one who had confidence issues, the one who had lost weight and had only begun to find who she was. I was a strong, independent woman who had taken control of her life a long, long time ago. I didn't need Eddie to tell me how to live my life, I didn't need him for validation.

I didn't need him for anything.

I was the new, improved Marissa Jones. I liked her, and I wanted her to stay.

"Marissa, I don't know what your relationship with Eddie was like in the past, all I know is you're someone I admire, someone who knows her own mind, even if you've been a little flaky in your quest to find The One." She smiled at me. "I hope you don't mind me saying that."

"I guess I have been." I looked down at my hands. "It's just . . . I was so in love with Eddie for so long, and he . . . he left me," I choked as tears ran down my cheeks.

It explained everything. If I loved someone, they would leave me.

Period. Maybe that's what I'd been running from, that's why I'd been so committed to not being committed?

What a total waste of time.

Bailey put her hand on mine. "Nash seemed like a good guy. Maybe you could give him another chance?"

Nash. I scrunched my eyes shut as a pang of guilt slammed into me. Nash had been nothing but a fantastic boyfriend to me. He was thoughtful, he was sweet, and he was kind—but most of all, he had let me be me. And how had I treated him in return? By leaving him because he wasn't Eddie.

Oh, no. What had I done?

"Honey?" Bailey asked, her face full of concern. "I hope I haven't gone too far. I have a habit of doing that."

I let out a puff of air. "No, no, you haven't." I shook my head, my mind speeding like it was competing in a NASCAR race. Eddie was wrong for me, I could see that as clear as glass. Nash, it was Nash. He was The One. And I'd totally messed it up.

"Marissa?"

I looked at Bailey and saw the concern clouding her face, and in that instant I knew what I wanted to do, what I *had* to do.

I locked my jaw. "I've made a mistake. A terrible, terrible mistake," I muttered, clasping my hands together. I looked at Bailey. "I need to fix it. I have to go. Do you mind?"

"Well, I was looking forward to a fun night out with you, but—" She chuckled. "You go, do what you need to do. And I'm kinda hoping I know what it is." She flashed me her brilliant smile, and I couldn't have suppressed my grin if my life had depended on it.

"Thanks, Bailey. You're the best." I took another sip of my drink for Dutch courage and stood up. I put my hand on Bailey's shoulder. "You've helped me see something I was totally blind to."

She shrugged, grinning. "All in a day's work."

"Will you be okay?"

"No worries. I've always got Buff over there, if I need some company." She nodded at the bar, and Buff smiled and raised his chin at her. She returned her attention to me. "You go get him."

I nodded, swallowing. I knew what my heart had been trying to tell me, but it had got all mixed up with my unresolved feelings for Eddie.

Nash was my Last First Date. And now I needed to try my best to get him back.

CHAPTER 20

I stood in front of the door, working hard at getting up my nerve. I needed to see him; I had things to say.

I raised my hand to knock, pausing in midair. What would he say? How would he react? Would I lose my nerve?

Before I could change my mind, I rapped my knuckles against the wooden door.

I waited. And waited. I could hear footsteps inside, and then the door swung open.

"Marissa!"

"Hey, Eddie," I replied, forcing a smile. "Someone let me into your building. I hope that's okay?"

"Of course!" He pulled me in for a kiss. "This is a wonderful surprise. I thought you were going to have a quiet night at home."

I stepped across the threshold and into his apartment. "Yes, well, I was, and then I needed to see you."

"Oh, that's so great." He beamed at me and I had to look away.

"Can we talk?" I asked, trying to swallow down the lump in my throat.

"Sure, babe, sure," he cooed, closing the door to his apartment behind me and leading me by my hand through the cavernous room to his large, white sofa.

"Is everything okay?" he asked, his face etched in concern.

I took a deep breath and nodded at him. "I . . . I need to tell you something."

"You've got me worried."

I bit my lip. This last week with Eddie had shown me so much about him and about me—and I didn't think he would like any of it very much. But I needed to say it, I needed for him to hear it—and I needed to hear it myself.

"I've changed," I began, the sadness beginning to dissipate a fraction inside. "I'm not the girl I was back when we were dating."

He nodded, reaching for my face. "I know. You're even more amazing now."

I placed my hand on his wrist and lowered his hand. I couldn't say what I needed to say with a guy's hand placed possessively on my cheek.

"Eddie, when we were dating back then I had such low self-esteem. I'd only just started to learn who I was, who I wanted to be."

He shrugged. "We were young."

"More than that, I was lost. You were so good for me in so many ways." He smiled at me. "And so bad, too." His face dropped. "Eddie, I'm my own person. I make my own decisions. I have a career and friends and a place in the world."

He narrowed his eyes at me. "What are you saying?"

"I guess I'm saying, I don't need you anymore. I thought I did, but I don't."

"But, I love you and you love me. Whatever this whole 'kick-ass girl' thing is you've got going on now"—he gestured at me as though I were an object—"I still want to be with you."

"You want to be with me despite me being a 'kick-ass girl'?" I asked, my eyes agog.

"Well, not if you put it that way. That makes me sound like a total ass."

I pushed myself up off the sofa, my inner "kick-ass girl" standing tall. "In some ways, you are a total ass, Eddie. And I'm not going to sit around while you pursue your dreams and disregard mine. It's not going to happen."

"But . . . but you can't do this to me!" He stood up to his full six-foot height, putting his hands on my shoulders. "This has been the best week of our lives."

I shook my head. "I'm sorry, not for me, but it has been a really valuable lesson." My heart softened a little. I had just called the man I'd been in love with for years an "ass." The least I could do was try to let him down gently now. "I didn't mean for this to happen. Eddie, I was in love with you for so long. When I saw you at the Cozy Cottage, I thought you were my Prince Charming, come to save me."

"I *am* your Prince Charming," he said, stroking my cheek like I was his pet.

I held his hand by his wrist once more. I shook my head. "No, you're not. And you know something? I don't need a Prince Charming, and I don't need to be saved."

He looked at me in utter bewilderment, as though I had told him the sky wasn't blue.

And then, his face changed. "You're going back to that guy you were seeing, Nash."

Pain seared through my chest as I thought of Nash and me at the Cozy Cottage Jam. I had been so close to him, so happy. He had been my equal, the man for me, someone who saw me for who I was, not what they wanted me to be.

And I'd totally screwed it up.

"You're right," I acquiesced, a brick heavy in my belly.

"I knew it!" He slammed his fist into his hand, his lips thin with anger.

I shook my head. "But he's not my Prince Charming, either. He's the guy I've fallen for, the guy I want to be with. And even though he doesn't want me, I'm going to try my best to win him over."

"You're leaving me for someone who doesn't even want to be with you?" His eyes were wide.

I chewed the inside of my lip and nodded.

"That's the most pathetic thing I've ever heard," he scoffed, his face reddening. "You haven't changed, you'll never change." He spat his words at me like gunfire.

I stood, stock-still, unable to move, my nostrils flaring, my eyes narrowed.

"You're chasing a phantom, a ghost. This guy doesn't want to be with you, just like *I* didn't want to be with you. But still you waited all those years, like the sad, pitiful person you are, hoping I'd change my mind." He peppered his words with spite—this man who had professed to love me only moments ago.

I could do without that kind of love.

I clenched my fists at my sides. This was not the way I'd seen this conversation going. But then, I hadn't been the one to break up with Eddie in the past. Perhaps he was always this bitter and nasty when a woman wised up to him?

Without a further word, I slipped the strap of my purse over my shoulder and began to walk toward the door.

"Oh, yeah, there you go. Go on, run to him, or rather, run back to your bedroom so you can obsess about him for what? Seven years?"

My hand on the doorknob, I turned to look at him, finally seeing him for what he was. He was so angry, I wouldn't have been surprised to see steam tooting out of his ears, his mouth frothing. I took a deep breath, knowing deep inside I had done the right thing. "Goodbye, Eddie."

"Yeah, whatever!" He threw his hands in the air and turned his back to me.

I pulled the door open and stepped out into the hallway, letting out a relieved sigh, pulling it shut behind me. As if I needed any further validation, that conversation drove the nails irrevocably into the coffin of our relationship.

I walked steadily down the hall to the elevator, proud of what I had done. I had stood up to the man who had wanted to keep me down.

I had been true to myself, and there was no turning back.

CHAPTER 21

I slumped out of Eddie's apartment building onto the street, jabbing at my phone to order an Uber. I had no clue where Nash would be on a Saturday evening, but I needed to find him and tell him how I felt.

I paced up and down the sidewalk, eager to put distance between Eddie and myself—and get to Nash as soon as I could. *Where is that Uber!* The bees in my belly were replaced by my old friends, the overexcited hamsters and that Destiny's Child song about survival became my theme song. I was a survivor, I wasn't "gon" give up.

I was going to get Nash back if it was the last thing I did.

A hybrid vehicle slid up to the curb after what felt like an hour of pacing like a caged tiger. Relieved I was finally making progress, I clambered in the back seat and the driver drove off. I figured it was still early enough that if Nash had plans tonight, he may still be at his home. The car pulled up outside Nash's place, and my belly flip-flopped when I noticed a couple of lights on inside in the evening dusk.

He was home.

At Nash's front door, I paused, taking some deep breaths in a vain attempt to quell my nerves. What was he going to say? Had I hurt him too much for him to take me back? Or, had he missed me and would greet me with open arms?

I did a silent prayer for the last option, raised my hand, and knocked on the door. I held my breath and waited. And waited. I knocked again, louder this time. *He has to be here!*

I heard the sound of a door opening, and my heart leapt into my mouth. This was it. This was my moment.

The door swung open and there Nash stood, looking at me in surprise.

"Hi," I managed, my heart beating so loudly in my ears it almost drowned me out.

His eyes narrowed. "What are you doing here?" His voice was hard, angry.

"I . . ." In all the time I'd had on my way to Nash's place, I hadn't worked out what I was going to say to him. I'd only got as far as, "Take me back!" And, I admit, I had hoped that would be enough.

He raised his eyebrows in expectation.

"Can I come in?" I asked.

He crossed his arms and shook his head. He might not have been friendly, but at least he hadn't slammed the door in my face. I was hanging on to anything I could.

I heard a puppy's excited bark, and my eyes darted to the door. What I wouldn't have done to have a time machine and zap myself back to when I was sitting on Nash's sofa, dogs everywhere. Before Eddie, before I broke up with Nash, making the biggest mistake of my life.

Nash didn't move. Instead, he stood, holding the door in one hand, glaring at me.

I chewed the inside of my lip. I wasn't giving up hope. "Okay. I get it, you're angry. And I don't blame you. But can you at least hear me out?"

His handsome face was hard, his jaw locked. "You've got two minutes."

So, no invitation inside. Got it.

I nodded. It was now or never. I needed to find the words that would soften his heart, that would allow him to forgive, that would bring him back to me.

I swallowed, hard. "I'm so sorry. I totally messed up. I . . . I thought Eddie and I were meant to be together, but I was wrong, so, so wrong. We're not. He's . . . well, he's not the man I thought he was. It's over." I took a step closer to him, my heart hammering even louder.

He didn't move a muscle, his narrowed eyes trained on me, silent.

"Do you think . . . we could try again?" I held my breath, hopeful.

"Try again?" he repeated, his brow knitted together.

"Please?" I took another step closer and reached out for his hand. As my fingers found his, he flinched, stepping back from me.

"Why?" He shook his head. "Why would I do that to myself, Marissa?"

"Because . . . because we were good together and . . . and I think I'm falling for you. In fact, I know I am. Nash, I . . . I love you."

He let out a short, sharp laugh. "You've fallen in love with me?" He shook his head, stroking his chin. "You have the weirdest way of showing it, you know that, right?"

My bottom lip trembled, and I hung my head, thoroughly ashamed of my behavior toward him. I knew I had treated him badly, I knew I probably didn't deserve a second chance with him, but I wanted him, oh, so much.

I had never felt this way about a man.

I looked back up at him and pushed my hair behind my ears. "You're right. I haven't treated you well. But please give me another chance. I've changed, I . . . I know things about myself I didn't know before, and I want to make this work . . . with you."

My speech over, I stood, waiting, the bees, the hamsters, a veritable menagerie of creatures, racing around my belly. He *had* to take me back. I knew how I felt about him; I knew it was love. Surely, he must have felt it too?

Eventually, he pressed his lips together. He shook his head. "No."

My mouth dropped open. Did he really just turn me down? "No?"

He shook his head again. "It's too late, Marissa. I . . . I can't."

189

I tried to swallow, my mouth as dry as a sandpit. Inside, my heart was breaking in two.

A puppy barked, and my eyes darted to the door beside him once more. "How are the pups?" I asked, desperate to stay with him, for our conversation not to be over—even if his words were killing me.

His face softened. "They're good. I've managed to find homes for a couple of them."

"Lucky?" I whispered, not sure I wanted to hear his response.

"No, not yet. I'm taking her and the other two to the SPCA soon. Hopefully, they'll find them good homes." His face was humorless, blank, impossible to read.

"Oh." I thought of the conversation we'd had about the number of dogs that needed homes—and the number whose lives were ended if such homes didn't eventuate. "Can I at least say goodbye?" I asked, my bottom lip betraying me as tears welled in my eyes.

He studied my face for a long moment, then silently stood back to let me step into the hall. With shaking legs and a pain in my heart, I stepped over the threshold, breathing in the familiar scent of Nash's home. I waited until he had closed the front door, then I opened the door to the living room. Two of the remaining puppies, Lucky included, were so close to the door, I almost banged into them as I pushed it open.

I crouched down with tears blurring my vision, patting the two dogs and telling them how beautiful they were. The third puppy came bounding over to us, jumping up Nash's leg. When Nash wasn't forthcoming with his affections—*I know how you feel, puppy*—he turned his attention to me, climbing on me and licking my ears along with Lucky and her litter mate.

I wiped my tears away and looked up at Nash. He was still watching me closely. "They've grown so much."

"That happens with puppies."

I smiled at him and I was sure I detected a hint of a smile on his face, but it was gone in a heartbeat.

Two of the puppies bounded across the floor, back to their mother, leaving Lucky, nuzzling me and trying to lick my face. I looked down into her big brown eyes, my heart melting at the sight of her. "Goodbye, little girl," I said, my voice choking as my heart broke afresh. "I'm going to miss you."

Lucky gave me a final lick, her tail still wagging a mile a minute. With the brick in the pit of my stomach, I placed her on the floor and watched her scamper over to Nash. He collected her up in his arms.

"Well, I suppose I had better get going. Unless . . .?" I bit my lip, holding my breath, my eyes trained on Nash. He still had Lucky in his arms, looking every inch the stoic dog rescuer he was.

His eyes met mine, and he held my gaze for a beat, two. And then he looked away from me, and I knew he was lost to me. "Yeah, you'd better get going."

And *thud*, my heart dropped to the floor, shattering into a million pieces.

It was done. Nash had made his decision. He didn't want me.

I nodded, not trusting myself to speak. I took the few shaky steps to the door and placed my trembling hand on his arm. I looked from Lucky's liquid brown eyes up into Nash's. "I'm sorry," I whispered, tears flowing down my cheeks, feeling the sting of regret with every fiber of my being.

He looked away from me, his jaw locked.

With a lump the size of Texas in my throat and tears streaming down my face, I pulled the living room door open and immediately closed it behind me. I stood for a moment, my mouth dropped open, a brick in my belly, trying to process what had just happened.

It was over.

And it was all my fault.

CHAPTER 22

*A*fter weeks of practice and ever-building excitement, mingled with a healthy serving of first-time nerves, the Cozy Cottage Jam Open Mic was finally here.

Bailey and Paige had allowed me after-hours access to the café last night, so I was able to practice my song in the very spot I would be delivering it soon. I had sat on the stool, the strap of my guitar slung over my shoulder, and sung my heart out. And it had felt *good*. Of course, I had sung to an empty room, but for Paige, who had been good to her word and stayed hidden from my view in the kitchen.

I glanced around the entranceway to the kitchen, out at the café. It had begun to fill up and I stood, my hands clasped, shifting my weight from foot to foot, running over the words to the song in my head.

Take me into your loving arms, kiss me under the light of a . . .

Wait, was it a thousand stars or a million stars? Or was it the stars and the moon?

"I'm getting it right now," Bailey said as she walked through the door, empty tray in her hands. She glanced at me as she placed the tray on the counter. "Nervous?"

"A little," I lied.

"You'll do great." She walked into the pantry at the back of the kitchen, emerging a moment later with a pre-prepared plate of snack food.

"I hope so. I only wish—" I bit my lip, thinking of the one person I wanted here the most tonight, the person who never wanted to see me again: Nash.

"Wish what?" Bailey asked.

I swallowed, my mouth dry. "I don't know. This whole thing was . . . well, it was Nash's idea."

Saying his name still hit me like a wrecking ball. He hadn't returned any of my texts, apologizing for what I had done and asking for his forgiveness. I had even sent him a basket of chew toys and dog treats, but I'd never heard a word.

I let out a nervous breath. Without Nash, I wouldn't be standing here, waiting to sing to a roomful of strangers.

"Honey, you need to focus on singing that song as best you can. That's all that matters right now." Bailey picked up her plate and paused, smiling at me. "And you're going to do great. You got this."

I returned her smile, bees buzzing in my belly. "I hope so."

Paige burst into the room, Cassie trailing behind her, almost knocking the plate out of Bailey's hands. "Sorry!" Paige exclaimed, steadying it.

"That was a close one," Bailey replied. She turned and winked at me before heading through the doorway, out into the café now humming with chatter.

"So, are you all set?" Paige asked, her face bright.

"I guess," I replied, convincing absolutely no one.

"Oh, you're going to be amazing."

"I have some news that might help," Cassie said with a wry grin.

"You do?" Hope rose inside me like a helium balloon. Nash must be here! He'd come after all. Happiness spread through my belly.

"I got a call only a few minutes ago. Apparently, Steve Bryant came in with a better offer at the last minute." She watched me, waiting for my reaction.

I furrowed my brow. Steve Bryant? Why would I care about Steve Bryant? And what did he have to do with Nash?

"Well? Aren't you happy?" Cassie asked when I didn't react.

I shook my head. "I'm sorry, what?"

"We lost Pukeko Chocolates to Telco! Steve Bryant and his team offered them some deal they said they couldn't refuse."

"They did?" Ordinarily, I would be infuriated by such news. But not this time. A smile spread across my face. "Poor Antoinette."

Cassie grinned. "I know, right?"

Paige interrupted us. "Everyone's sitting and we're about to begin. You good to go?"

I nodded as the bees tried to escape up my throat. I swallowed them down. I wanted to do this. No, scratch that, I *needed* to do this.

Since my realization I had been in love with a phantom all these years, and that I was no longer that sad, lonely girl I once was, desperate for validation, I had been determined to do what I had set out to do, to 'follow my passion,' as Nash had called it.

And like with my singing, I was not going to give up hope of getting Nash back one day. I was Marissa Jones, and I could achieve anything.

You see, I knew Nash was The One. I just knew. And he was going to be, one day.

I hadn't heard hide nor tail from Eddie, and that suited me just fine. I had noticed his Facebook status had changed from "single" to "it's complicated," and I was proud to report it hadn't affected me in the least. I only hoped the woman he was being "complicated" with now had the strength of character I had lacked when we were together and stands up to him to ensure she got what she wanted.

But, he was no longer my problem.

"Okay, I'll go out and announce you," Paige said. With an encouraging smile, she left the kitchen.

"Knock 'em dead," Cassie said before disappearing through the doorway herself.

I took a deep breath and peered around the doorway once more. I spotted Will, Josh, and Ryan, sitting at a table at the back of the café. Ryan looked over toward me, smiled, and gave me the thumbs-up. I smiled back, bolstered by Cassie's news.

I could do this!

I watched as Paige made her way to the makeshift stage. She stood in front of the microphone in the corner, a stool behind her. "Ladies and gentlemen, hi!" She smiled her gorgeous smile, and the audience smiled and clapped, some calling out greetings in response.

"Welcome to the first ever Cozy Cottage Jam Open Mic! We at the Cozy Cottage Café are so happy to have you all here tonight, and I hope you've come ready to dazzle us with your musical performances. Now, a few rules: one song each, no heckling, and keep it clean, people."

I collected my guitar from its spot, leaning up against the kitchen the wall, and held it in my now clammy hands.

"So, first up we have a Cozy Cottage regular, the fabulous Marissa Jones!" The audience clapped, and I could hear Will catcalling from the back, just as he had threatened to do.

I stepped out from the sanctity of behind the counter and walked through the audience in my favorite pair of heels over to the stage, my nerves pinging around my body like a ball in a pinball machine. I pulled out the stool and sat down, putting my guitar on my lap and adjusting the microphone.

"Hey, everyone," I said, looking out at the sea of faces. The café wasn't that large, but Paige and Bailey had brought in extra seating, so there must have been a good few dozen people in the audience tonight. I tried not to think about it.

I strummed my guitar, ensuring it was in tune, although I knew it was as I'd tuned it only moments ago. I glanced up at the sea of faces once more, my tummy in knots. They were sitting in expectation, watching me. I swallowed.

There was nothing left to do but sing.

I leaned into the microphone again. "Ah . . . this song is for someone who couldn't be here tonight, but who I wish . . . was." A wave of sadness rolled over me, and I did my best to ignore it, instead turning my attention to the position of my fingers on my guitar.

Without further delay, I strummed the first few bars and launched into the love song. I had chosen it to sing to Nash, to tell him how I felt about him, the man who had encouraged me to overcome my fears.

Now, I was singing it to my friends and a roomful of strangers, Nash nowhere to be seen.

As I sang the lyrics to the song, I closed my eyes, my nervousness simply slipping away. "When your legs don't work . . ." It was like it was just me and my guitar, nothing and no one else. The melody flowed, and as I sang about falling in love, about being in love, I knew. No matter how, no matter when, I had to get Nash back. Pure and simple. He was my Last First Date.

As I sang the last line and strummed the last bar, I opened my eyes and smiled tentatively. I had done it. I had no idea what I had sounded like, whether I was even any good, but I had done it. The audience burst into applause, and my smile grew until it filled my face, my heart bursting with pride.

"Thanks," I said, a little embarrassed but so thoroughly proud of myself. I stood up and leaned down to the microphone once more. "I'd like to say I'll be here all week, but that was definitely a one-off."

As I straightened up, I spotted a familiar face, watching me intently from just inside the front door.

Nash.

My heart leapt into my mouth at the sight of him. *What is he doing here?* I shook my head and blinked. He was still there, I hadn't imagined it.

I looked at Paige, standing next to me. She shot me a quizzical look.

"Sorry, I . . . I'll get off your stage," I managed. With shaking legs, I walked past her, my head full to the brim of what this might mean.

As Paige announced the next performer from her clipboard, I looked over at Nash once more. He was still watching me with a look I couldn't read. I chewed the inside of my lip, my breathing rapid. He nodded toward the counter, and I swallowed, nodding back.

A moment later, we stood, facing one another as the next performer broke into a famous Motown number and the crowd hooted with excitement.

"Hi," I said, my voice breathless as I clutched onto the neck of my guitar.

"Hi." He nodded, pressing his lips together. Try as I might, his face was impossible to read. "Can we . . .?" He nodded at the kitchen.

"Sure." I lifted the counter leaf and stepped around, past the register, and out into the kitchen. Nash followed.

Bailey looked up at me from a cake she was frosting. "Marissa, you were amazing!" she said, her face aglow. She glimpsed behind me, looking straight at Nash. "Oh." She straightened up. "Look, just give me one moment."

"Please, don't let us interrupt you. This is your kitchen," Nash said. "Let's go out the back," he said to me.

I nodded and concentrated on putting one foot in front of the other, heading to the door. With unsteady hands, I placed my guitar up against the wall. It slipped, and I caught it.

"Here," Nash said, taking it from me and placing it in a secure spot.

"Thanks," I mumbled, wishing my hands hadn't let me down.

Once outside, under the light of a full moon, I stopped and turned, looking directly at Nash. I had no clue what he was doing here, but I couldn't help but hope it was for a very good reason, the best reason.

"You were great," he said without a smile.

I pressed my lips together, the hamsters doing cartwheels in my belly. "Thanks."

He stared at me, his jaw twitching.

I shifted my weight. *It's now or never, Marissa.* "I sang that song . . . for you."

He nodded. "Thank you."

Wow, what every girl wanted to hear when she told a guy she had overcome crippling nerves to stand up in front of an audience and sing him a love song: "thank you."

Again, he stood in front of me, not saying a word, simply staring at me.

"Did you want to talk about anything or . . . something?" I asked, hoping to break whatever *this* was.

"Yeah, I do."

"Okay," I led. Was it me or was this getting beyond awkward? I decided to take a punt. I mean, he had to be here for a reason, and I hoped with all my heart that reason was a good one. I clutched my hands and took a cautious step toward him. He didn't move. My heart was hammering hard. "Look, Nash. I know you're probably still mad at me, and I totally understand why, but can —"

Without a word, he stepped closer to me, swept me up in his arms, and pressed his lips against mine, kissing me as though his life depended on it. And oh, my, did I kiss him back, clutching onto him, barely believing he was here with me.

We pulled apart, panting. I had to blink. There were stars, lots of them, and I didn't mean just in the sky.

"Wha-what?"

He fixed me with his electric eyes. "No more freak-outs, okay? No more exes turning up out of the blue. Just you and me."

My chest expanded, my breath caught in my throat as my whole body came out in goosebumps. Just Nash and me. "You want to be with me?"

He nodded and then leaned in and brushed his lips against mine in such a way as to leave no room for any doubt. I wrapped my arms around him and pulled him in tight.

He chuckled. "Marissa, I want to be with you. I love you."

I looked into his eyes, my heart swelling. "I love you, too."

"That song." He sighed. "You were amazing."

"I was?" I flushed with pride.

"Remind me never to take you on in karaoke." He chuckled. "I'm really proud of you." We grinned at one another.

Nash was back, and he loved me. I had overcome my fears and sung a song to an audience. And I knew myself better than I ever had. And you know what? I kinda liked me.

* * *

AFTER THE LAST song had been sung and the Cozy Cottage Jam Open Mic was officially over, Nash and I stood hand-in-hand on the street together outside the Cozy Cottage Café, looking in. We had spent the last hour and a half, sitting in his truck, talking, kissing, planning, kissing, and kissing some more. We had a lot of time to make up, and kissing Nash had officially become one of my favorite things to do of all time.

And it had felt so good, so right. Unlike Eddie, Nash was completely supportive of me. He liked me for me, not as someone to bolster his own self-interest. As we talked, a sense of calm, of knowing pervaded me. I knew he was the man for me, no question. And he'd come back to me, after all my mess ups.

I could barely believe my luck.

I spotted movement at the back of the café. I knocked on the window, and Cassie appeared from the kitchen, a puzzled look on her face. A moment later, Paige followed her out. She walked over and unlocked the door, letting us in.

"Oh, my! You guys! Does this mean . . .?" she asked, her eyes wide.

I looked up at Nash and we shared a smile. Squeezing his hand, I replied, "It does."

Paige squealed, jumping up and down on the spot. "Hey, guys! Get out here!" she called over her shoulder.

Cassie gave both of us a hug, congratulating us both on our fine choice.

"You were my pick all along," she said to Nash, and he smiled back at her.

The rest of the gang filed out of the kitchen: Josh, Will, Bailey, and to my surprise, my brother, Ryan, looking happier than I'd seen him since the last time we were at the Cozy Cottage together, that fateful night when Eddie had come back into my life.

"Does this mean you're dating again?" Bailey asked with hope in her eyes.

I stole a quick glance at Nash who smiled back at me, his face soft. "It does."

Bailey hugged me and then moved on to Nash, asking him if he had heard me sing.

Ryan took the opportunity to sidle up to me and ask in a low voice, "Are you happy?"

I nodded, my smile broad. My heart was full. "Oh, yes."

"Well, then, I'm happy for you. For both of you."

I regarded him through narrowed eyes. "What's happened to 'doomed love' and all that?"

He shrugged. "I don't know. It's getting old, I guess."

I smiled at him. There was hope for him yet. "Does this mean I'm getting my sofa back soon?"

He scrunched up his nose. "Maybe?"

"Good. You deserve to be happy."

"Marissa? Do you want to do the thing?" Nash asked, interrupting us.

"Oh, that sounds interesting," Cassie said, her eyes bright.

I grinned at Nash. "Okay. I'll be right back, everyone."

Nash pulled his keys out of his pocket, and I pulled the door open, heading to his truck. A few moments later, I returned, knocking on the door to be let back in.

Bailey opened the door and immediately looked down at my feet. "And what do we have here?"

I leaned down and scooped the ball of fluff at my feet up into my arms. "This is Lucky." Nash wrapped his arm around my waist and pulled me into him as Lucky proceeded to lick my neck, her tail fanning my friends.

"Oh, my!" Cassie exclaimed, her hand flying to her face. "That is the cutest thing I ever saw!" She patted Lucky. "You are the sweetest."

Paige and Bailey followed suit, patting Lucky who lapped their attention right up.

"When I go on my Last First Date, I want one of these, too. A package deal: great man and cute puppy." Lucky tried to lick her hand as she stroked her head.

"Dude, you turned up to win your woman with a *puppy*?" Josh asked as he shook his head. Turning to Will and Ryan, he added, "We've got to work on our game, guys."

"It's just the way I roll," Nash said with a smile, winking at me.

"Well, whatever it is, you three make the perfect little family," Paige said with a sigh, her hand on her heart.

With Lucky in my arms, I looked up at Nash, my heart full to the brim. My face broke into a smile as wide as the Pacific Ocean. Not that long ago a statement like that would have had me running for the hills.

Not anymore.

Now, I was no longer committed to not being committed. I knew where my home was, I knew my own heart. And I was the luckiest girl in the world.

THE END

ACKNOWLEDGMENTS

I *loved* writing Marissa's story! Giving her depth beyond her witty quips and self-assuredness in the first two books in the *Cozy Cottage Café* series was such a pleasure, and I hope you enjoyed getting to know her as much as I did writing her story.

I have a list of people to thank for helping me bring this book to publication. As always, thank you to my editor, Chrissy Wolfe from The Every Free Chance Reader. Chrissy, you 'get' my writing and help me make it so much better. Thank you!

For this book, I have gained two wonderful critique partners. Jackie Rutherford, your quick wit and sense of humor are always appreciated, and you can spot a storyline flaw at one hundred paces. Kirsty McManus is more than a critique partner. She also helped me get this book done, with daily writing total check ins and constant cheer-leading. Kirsty, your attention to detail is almost not human, and your support of my writing gives me wings. I know I'm in very safe hands with you two by my side.

Thank you to my beta reading team, especially Leanne Mackay, who always has astute observations and immensely useful feedback for me.

Thank you also to Sue Traynor for designing yet another stunning cover for me. Sue, you get it right each time, and I thank you for it.

Thank you to my key writers' groups, Chick Lit Chat HQ and the Hawke's Bay ladies of the Romance Writers of New Zealand group. Writing is a profession like few others, and your support is invaluable.

This wouldn't be an acknowledgements section without mentioning my family. My husband and son are both so supportive of me. I love you both for it so much and I'm lucky to have you. I would also like to thank my mother-in-law. Robyn, you are so proud of me and my writing, and I want you to know how much it means to me.

Last but certainly not least, thank you to all my readers. I hope I can keep writing books you can fall in love with.

ABOUT THE AUTHOR

Kate O'Keeffe is a *USA TODAY* bestselling and award-winning author who writes exactly what she loves to read: laugh-out-loud romantic comedies with swoon-worthy heroes and gorgeous feel-good happily ever afters. She lives and loves in beautiful Hawke's Bay, New Zealand with her family and two scruffy but loveable dogs.

When she's not penning her latest story, Kate can be found hiking up hills (slowly), traveling to different countries around the globe, and eating chocolate. A lot of it.